HAPPY HOLIDAYS

www.**randomhousechildrens**.co.uk

HAVE YOU READ THEM ALL?

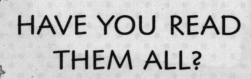

WHERE TO START

THE DINOSAUR'S PACKED LUNCH
THE MONSTER STORY-TELLER

FOR YOUNGER READERS

BURIED ALIVE!
CLIFFHANGER
GLUBBSLYME
LIZZIE ZIPMOUTH
SLEEPOVERS
THE CAT MUMMY
THE MUM-MINDER
THE WORRY WEBSITE

FIRST CLASS FRIENDS

BAD GIRLS
BEST FRIENDS
SECRETS
VICKY ANGEL

HISTORICAL ADVENTURES

OPAL PLUMSTEAD
QUEENIE
THE LOTTIE PROJECT

ALL ABOUT JACQUELINE WILSON

JACKY DAYDREAM
MY SECRET DIARY

FAMILY DRAMAS

CANDYFLOSS
CLEAN BREAK
COOKIE
FOUR CHILDREN AND IT
LILY ALONE
LITTLE DARLINGS
LOLA ROSE
MIDNIGHT
THE BED AND BREAKFAST STAR
THE ILLUSTRATED MUM
THE LONGEST WHALE SONG
THE SUITCASE KID
KATY

MOST POPULAR CHARACTERS

HETTY FEATHER
SAPPHIRE BATTERSEA
EMERALD STAR
DIAMOND
THE STORY OF TRACY BEAKER
THE DARE GAME
STARRING TRACY BEAKER

STORIES ABOUT SISTERS

DOUBLE ACT
THE BUTTERFLY CLUB
THE DIAMOND GIRLS
THE WORST THING
ABOUT MY SISTER

FOR OLDER READERS

DUSTBIN BABY
GIRLS IN LOVE
GIRLS IN TEARS
GIRLS OUT LATE
GIRLS UNDER PRESSURE
KISS
LOVE LESSONS
MY SISTER JODIE

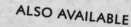

ALSO AVAILABLE

PAWS AND WHISKERS
THE JACQUELINE WILSON
CHRISTMAS CRACKER
THE JACQUELINE WILSON TREASURY

☆ ABOUT THE AUTHOR ☆

Jacqueline Wilson is one of Britain's bestselling
authors, with more than 35 million books sold
in the UK alone. She has been honoured with
many prizes for her work, including the Guardian
Children's Fiction Award and the Children's Book
of the Year. Jacqueline is a former Children's
Laureate, a professor of children's literature,
and in 2008 she was appointed a Dame for
services to children's literacy.

Visit Jacqueline's fantastic website at
www.jacquelinewilson.co.uk

Jacqueline Wilson

HAPPY HOLIDAYS

ILLUSTRATED BY
NICK SHARRATT

CORGI

JACQUELINE WILSON'S HAPPY HOLIDAYS
A CORGI BOOK 978 0 440 87098 2

HOLIDAYS
By Jacqueline Wilson
Extract from THE JACQUELINE WILSON
SUMMER HOLIDAY JOURNAL
First published by Doubleday, 2013
Text copyright © Jacqueline Wilson, 2013
Illustrations copyright © Nick Sharratt, 2013

HOLIDAYS
By Nick Sharratt
Extract from THE JACQUELINE WILSON
SUMMER HOLIDAY JOURNAL
First published by Doubleday, 2013
Text copyright © Nick Sharratt, 2013
Illustrations copyright © Nick Sharratt, 2013

TRACY BEAKER'S BIG DAY OUT
First published in Girl Talk Magazine, 1999
Text copyright © Jacqueline Wilson, 1999
Illustrations copyright © Nick Sharratt, 2015

MY SUMMER HOLIDAY
First published by Corgi, 2015
Text copyright © Jacqueline Wilson, 2015
Illustrations copyright © Nick Sharratt, 2015

BURIED ALIVE!
First published by Doubleday, 1998
Text copyright © Jacqueline Wilson, 1998
Illustrations copyright © Nick Sharratt and Sue Heap, 1998

HETTY FEATHER'S HOLIDAY
Extract from SAPPHIRE BATTERSEA
First published by Doubleday, 2011
Text copyright © Jacqueline Wilson, 2011
Illustrations copyright © Nick Sharratt, 2011

WHAT'S THE COUNTRY?
First published in MORE MUCK AND MAGIC (Egmont)
Text copyright © Jacqueline Wilson, 2001
Illustrations copyright © Nick Sharratt, 2012

BEAUTY'S HOLIDAY
Extract from COOKIE
First published by Doubleday, 2008
Text copyright © Jacqueline Wilson, 2008
Illustrations copyright © Nick Sharratt, 2008

GEMMA'S HOLIDAY
Extract from BEST FRIENDS
First published by Doubleday, 2008
Text copyright © Jacqueline Wilson, 2008
Illustrations copyright © Nick Sharratt, 2008

OUR FREE DAY OUT
First published in THE JACQUELINE
WILSON SUMMER ANNUAL
Text copyright © Jacqueline Wilson, 2011
Illustrations copyright © Nick Sharratt, 2011

First published as JACQUELINE WILSON'S HAPPY HOLIDAYS by Corgi, 2015
an imprint of Random House Children's Publishers UK
A Penguin Random House Company

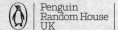

Penguin
Random House
UK

5 7 9 10 8 6

MIX
Paper from
responsible sources
FSC
www.fsc.org
FSC® C016897

Set in New Century Schoolbook LT

Random House Children's Publishers UK,
61–63 Uxbridge Road, London W5 5SA

www.randomhousechildrens.co.uk
www.totallyrandombooks.co.uk
www.randomhouse.co.uk

Addresses for companies within The Random House Group Limited
can be found at: www.randomhouse.co.uk/offices.htm

THE RANDOM HOUSE GROUP Limited Reg. No. 954009

A CIP catalogue record for this book is available from the British Library.

Printed and bound in Great Britain by CPI Group (UK) Ltd, Croydon CR0 4YY

☆ CONTENTS ☆

☆ HOLIDAYS ☆
by Jacqueline Wilson

I write a great deal about favourite holidays in *Jacky Daydream* and *My Secret Diary*. I loved going to the seaside, and the two most memorable holidays of my childhood were spent in Bournemouth and Newquay. I still like going to the seaside now – though the sea feels so freezing cold that I haven't got the courage to go in swimming any more. I like swimming in warm sea now! I recently had a fantastic holiday in Barbados where the turquoise water was just like jumping into a bath.

However, I think my all-time favourite holiday venue is Hay-on-Wye, which is nowhere near the sea. It's a tiny Victorian town in a valley on the Welsh Borders. It's magical countryside. There are gorgeous wild ponies up in the Black Mountains and you can see for miles if you stagger up the nearest bluff. The river Wye runs beside the town and there are lovely riverside walks and a beautiful spot called the Warren for picnics and paddles in the water.

Hay has fantastic restaurants and pubs and a wonderful ice-cream parlour, so I always go home feeling very fat. But the best thing of all about Hay-on-Wye is the thirty second-hand bookshops – my idea of bliss!

☆ HOLIDAYS ☆
by Nick Sharratt

I had a lot of great holidays when I was a boy, but if I had to choose I'd pick the first time we went camping, when I was about to turn eleven.

We started off with a few days in the Lake District where we pitched our brand-new tents (one for Mum and Dad, one for my sisters and one for my brother and me) on a campsite overlooking Derwentwater, and I just couldn't believe how spectacular the view was, with the glistening lake and the mountains in the background. Then we drove over to Northumberland, visited Hadrian's Wall and had a lazy day or two by the sea.

Finally we went to stay with some friends who had a cottage in the Yorkshire Dales, but not big enough for everyone, so the boys still slept in the tent. I'd thought the lakes were impressive, but for me Swaledale was complete paradise, a truly beautiful, utterly peaceful valley with grass so green it was almost luminous, hidden away like a secret among the wild moors. We went for long walks alongside the river Swale or scrabbled up the side valleys to cook fry-ups, swim in rock pools and peer into the mouths of the ruined lead mine tunnels up there. I fell completely in love with the place and it's still my absolute favourite destination for a holiday!

TRACY BEAKER'S BIG DAY OUT

Where are you going for your summer holiday? I'm jetting off to America. I'm going to Disneyland. I'm going on all the really scary rides, especially the one where you whizz up in a rocket and spin round and round. I'm going to go on that twice. I'm going to hold hands with Mickey Mouse and fly in the Dumbo plane. I love that film *Dumbo*, especially the bit where Dumbo twines trunks with his mum. I'd do that with my mum. If I had a trunk. If my mum ever came to see me.

She's a famous actress in Hollywood. She *is*. That's why she shoved me in this Children's Home. She's way too busy to look after me. I understand. I do really. Anyway, I'll get to see her on my summer holiday, won't I? That's where I'd *like* to go. Only they're so mean and boring in the Children's Home. They won't take us anywhere decent for a holiday. You'd think kids in Homes would get really great holidays seeing as we're deprived. Huh! Guess where we're *really* going?

 7

To this boring boring boring outdoor activity centre in the country. It's where we always go.

We do stuff like canoeing and abseiling and pony trekking. I thought it would be great but last year they kept picking on me. It wasn't fair. Just because I gave Justine and Louise's canoe a tweeny little flip with my paddles. I was just experimenting. They did the most amazing *submarine* canoeing before they surfaced, spluttering.

I got into even more trouble when we did abseiling. I couldn't understand why Weedy Peter and some of the little kids acted like they thought it was seriously scary. It was too easy-peasy for me. So I tried turning a somersault and descending upside down. It was mega-great – until I got in a tangle and ended tied up in knots. I was just being inventive. I didn't see why they had to read the riot act.

They had serious doubts about letting me do pony trekking. I promised to be as good as gold – and I *was*. I had this amazing black pony called Nightmare. I really loved her. I groomed her for hours, brushing her mane and her tail. I didn't even make a fuss about mucking out her stable.

I was the best rider. I really was. 'Look at Tracy,' they said. But after a while they stopped looking at me so I decided to liven things up a bit. I knew Nightmare was bored with all that prissy trotting. I thought it was time for a little gallop. So I dug my heels in and Nightmare hurtled forward, so fast that I shot off her back and ended up head first in a nettle-patch. That was a *real* nightmare.

So I'm not exactly looking forward to returning. And the guy who runs the centre probably won't be too thrilled when he catches sight of me.

I had a good long m-o-a-n about all this to Cam. She's going to be my foster mum. She *is*. This time it's really true. Cam's going to be my foster mum until my *own* mum finishes making her movies and we get it together again.

Cam's thrilled at the idea of fostering me. Well. She's given it serious thought. Perhaps she wasn't that keen just at first but now she's going to all these classes about being a good foster parent. It's a bit of a waste of time if you ask me. I know *exactly*

what a good foster parent should be like. She should let me sleep in every morning and take me to McDonald's every single day and let me watch horror movies on the telly till late into the night and she should buy me HUGE presents every day, double on my birthday – *and* take me for decent summer holidays. She's seeing me every week now with a view to fostering me after the summer. It's a shame she and my stupid social worker can't get their act together and get me fostered *during* the summer – and then Cam could take me to America.

'Dream on, Tracy,' said Cam. 'I'm having a bit of a cash flow problem. Like all my cash flows out of my purse and once I've paid my flat money and bought some food there's hardly any left.'

I like Cam but sometimes I wonder if she's the right foster mum for me. I really want one with lots and lots and lots of money. I mean, you can't have a good time without money, can you?

Well, maybe you can. Wait till I tell you!

Cam comes to see me every Saturday. We usually have this little routine. She takes me to McDonald's.

That's the best bit. Then we go for a trip somewhere. Nowhere exciting – mostly museums and art galleries. I don't mind dinosaurs and I like giggling at paintings of ladies with big fat bottoms – but it's mostly pretty boring.

But after I had my mega-holiday moan Cam rang me up at the Home and suggested that next Saturday we might have a *mini* holiday together – a special fun day out.

'Really? No museums? No art galleries? *Proper* fun?' I said.

'Absolutely,' said Cam.

'Can we go anywhere?'

'Well, within reason.'

'Right! I know where I want to go! We'll get the Eurostar to Paris and then we'll go to Disneyland and—'

'And that idea has to go on hold unless I just happen to win the Lottery,' Cam said firmly.

'Well . . . how about an amusement park over here? Chessington World of Adventures? Legoland?'

'Maybe towards the end of the summer. If I can manage it. But I was thinking more along the lines of a day at the seaside. My old auntie's got this beach hut. I used to love going there when I was your age.'

I pondered. 'So what would we do?'

'Swim.'

'Is there a pool?'

'In the sea!'

I wasn't at all sure about this idea.

'What else? Do we build sandcastles?'

'It's pebbles, actually.'

'Ah. So . . . we build piles of pebbles?'

Cam shook her head at me.

'I'll *throw* pebbles at you if you don't watch out! We just go to the seaside and enjoy ourselves. If you want.'

'I do want,' I said.

So I spent ages boasting to all the other kids about my Big Day Out. I said we were going to this amazing beach resort and we'd both loll in the sun drinking cocktails by our own private apartment. I was up at six on Saturday, dressed in my special Day Out at the Sea clothes – a little T-shirt that I'd cut with scissors till it resembled a dead cool crop top (well, sort of) and shorts (borrowed from Louise when she wasn't watching her wardrobe) and super stylish sunglasses that made me look like my mum the movie star.

There was just one problem. It was pouring with rain. Justine and Louise laughed meanly at breakfast and said I couldn't possibly go to the seaside now. I started to have an argument and then Louise suddenly recognized the shorts I was wearing and protested bitterly. I abandoned the argument and charged out the front door, still clutching my bread and butter breakfast.

Cam was just drawing up in her junky old car.

'Hi, Tracy! Lovely weather for ducks, eh?' she said, grinning ruefully.

'Can we still go?' I said.

'You bet,' said Cam. 'But you need to get some warmer clothes, don't you?'

'It'll brighten up by the time we get to the seaside,' I said, getting into the car.

So we set off. Cam had two bars of chocolate and a big bottle of Coke in the car so I had a second breakfast. I invented a brand new sandwich with my leftover bread and butter and milk chocolate – delicious! I felt as fizzy as the Coke. It was going to be a great day out. All we needed was the sun to come out.

The sun seemed to have spun off into a new galaxy altogether. Black clouds loomed above us all the way, and the rain was relentless. The windscreen wipers had to go slonk-slonk-slonk double quick to clear the screen.

'Who cares?' said Cam, and she slotted this tape of old rock music into her cassette player.

'Can we play it loud?' I asked. You're not allowed to turn the volume up in the Home because you disturb the babies.

'Loud as you like,' said Cam.

She started singing and I did too. We bellowed 'The sun ain't gonna shine any more . . .' – and it didn't.

But it didn't matter a bit. We could hardly *see* the sea when we got there. It was all dark grey – the sea, the sky, the cliffs, the pebbles on the beach. But the wooden beach huts were painted red and blue and green and yellow – and there was one magic one right at the end painted red orange yellow green blue indigo violet, just like a rainbow.

'Guess which is ours,' said Cam, grinning.

It *was* the rainbow one. Cam unlocked it. It was a bit poky and dusty inside, but kind of cute, like a little Wendy House. There was even a little stove with a kettle. Cam made herself a cup of her weird herbal tea and I had some more Coke. I wished there was a little fire as well as a little stove. Cam seemed to be hot as she took off her big jersey – so after a while I put it on. I looked a bit funny because it came right

14

down to my knees, but it didn't matter, it was just Cam and me. She got a bit goosebumpy in her T-shirt so she put her old aunty's padded jacket on. *She* looked funny too. She did a daft little dance inside the hut but she kept bumping into things so she opened the door and danced outside in the pouring rain. She looked even dafter – but it looked fun too, so I dashed out and boogied around too until we were both helpless with laughter and soaked to the skin.

'So let's go in swimming,' said Cam.

'In the rain?'

'Well, we're wet already, aren't we?'

'But we'll be freezing in the sea.'

'Not if we rush around and keep warm.'

'There are *things* though. Fish. Crabs.'

'Killer whales?' said Cam. 'Come on, I'll be Killer Woman and you be Killer Girl.' She started stripping down to her swimming costume.

'I haven't *got* a swimming costume.'

'Wear your knickers!' said Cam. 'Come on, last one in is a sissy!'

So we went in swimming. I discovered something strange. When it's ever so cold and rainy the water feels warmer. It was still cold enough to make me shriek getting in, but once I'd ducked down and got my shoulders wet it was suddenly fun, just the way Cam promised. We held hands and jumped the waves and

 15

then she swam for a bit while I rode on her shoulders, although we both kept capsizing.

It really *was* freezing when we came out but Cam rubbed us both dry in the beach hut and dressed me in her big jersey *and* her aunty's padded jacket until I stopped shivering. She made more herbal tea and I had some too, special strawberry flavour, and then we got stuck into the picnic proper. It wasn't quite McDonald's standard but I *quite* like cheese and salad rolls, and then I had bananas and grapes and a whole packet of Smarties, rainbow colours to match the beach hut!

Then we went for a long walk, still in the rain, looking at all the seagulls and collecting shells and seaweed. It was a little too much like Nature Study, but quite good fun. Then we went on the pier and that *was* fun. There weren't any really scary rides but we both went on this little kid's roundabout and then we went in the old arcade. There weren't any really good modern games but we won a troll doll for me on the cranes and then a tube of those baby soap bubbles.

Then we walked right up and over the cliffs, all on our own in the rain. We sang at the tops of our voices, sometimes making up the words as we went along. Then we went round to the fish and chip shop and got a big bag of chips each for our tea. They got a bit soggy as it was still pouring, but we didn't care.

Do you know something weird? The sun suddenly shone straight through the dark clouds just as we were getting in the car to go back. It was still raining though . . .

'So there must be a rainbow,' said Cam.

We both turned round and there it was, a big glowing arc in the sky.

We stood hand in hand, looking and looking, and then we drove back. I had the car window open and I blew rainbow bubbles all the way, watching them float up up up into the air.

So that was my Big Day Out – and do you know something? I haven't exaggerated a single word of it. I couldn't make it up better if I tried.

MY SUMMER HOLIDAY

If you ask me, I can't think of a worse subject, Mrs Spencer. Who wants to write about their summer holiday on the first day back at school? But all right, I'll give it a go.

The thing is, I was absolutely dreading going on holiday this year. I know you'll think that kinda weird. But then I'm mega certain you think I'm a totally weird kinda girl.

I have an even weirder family, believe you me. There's my mum for a start. She might come across as reasonably sane, and when she comes to parents' evening she'll dress up and act all concerned and sorrowful if you start bad-mouthing me like all the other teachers. But I tell you, she's barking mad. She must be, or she'd never have picked Silly Simon as my stepdad. I call him S.S. for short, and he acts like a

That's big of you, Hayley! I expect you to do your homework without comment!

There is no such word as 'kinda'. PLEASE try not to use silly slang in a school composition.

Inappropriate!

member of the S.S., forever bossing me about and telling me what to do. I can't stick him.

I'm not that keen on Keira either. She's my sister. Keira's only two years older than me, one year and eleven months actually, and yet she thinks she's got the perfect right to tell me what to do and generally patronize me. We have to share a bedroom which is totally unfair. She uses so much perfume and hairspray and stuff I practically choke to death, and she's always nag nag nagging because I leave all my stuff out. I just don't see the point when I'm going to get it out again the next day.

We have huge arguments about the posters on the walls too. She likes all these pathetic pop stars and moans about my glorious pictures of dogs. I get all these animal mags and cut out all the illustrations and stick them all over my two walls. I have carefully cut out photos of cute Chihuahuas and drawings of dotty Dalmatians and posters of perky poodles. There, Mrs Spencer, I know all about alliteration!

So I see!

I am absolutely crazy about dogs. And for years and years I haven't been able to have one for various totally lame reasons: we live in a flat; Mum's out at work all day; Keira imagines she's allergic to dog fur, etc, etc. But I have been campaigning for years and years for us to have a dog.

AND NOW WE HAVE ONE!!!!!!!!!!!

It was actually all down to Silly Simon, which is kinda irritating.

Try not to start a sentence with a conjunction — and I don't think we need so many exclamation marks. One will do!

He went down the pub and when he came home late he found this little abandoned puppy tied up to a railing. It was whimpering and whining and though S.S. is often a real pig to me I have to admit he is not totally heartless. He tucked the poor little puppy inside his jacket and took him home.

Oh dear, I'm finding your writing style EXTREMELY irritating, Hayley.

23

He was going to take him to Battersea Dogs and Cats Home in the morning – but I begged and pleaded and cried and *eventually* Mum and Simon gave in and said we could try looking after him just for a week. Oh, he was the dearest little boy in the world, with a black and white face and black dots speckling his back and black legs with white paws.

'OMG, he's a Dalmatian!' I said, utterly thrilled.

One Hundred and One Dalmatians is my all-time favourite film. I totally adore it. I've watched it at least fifty times. Even Keira liked it too when we were little, though now she makes out she doesn't like baby cartoons any more.

'Dalmatians are ever such expensive dogs,' I said. 'Wow, Simon, you couldn't have found a better puppy! What shall we call him? What's black and white? Bull's Eye sweets? Zebras? Them big birds? Yeah, let's call him Magpie!'

'Magpies are noisy and they steal things,' said Mum. 'If this little puppy does likewise you're not keeping him, Hayley!'

Try not to use that expression, Hayley – it's blasphemous and unpleasantly affected.

24

But Simon was so chuffed I'd said something nice to him for once that he actually took my side against Mum when the week was up. Unbelievably she wanted to take him to Battersea just because he'd done a few pees and poos on the carpet – *all* the carpets – and been sick on the cream sofa and chewed all the computer wires and eaten Mum's cardi and my shoe and Keira's dressing gown and most of the make-up in her handbag. I mean, he wasn't doing this on purpose, he was just a little puppy who didn't know any better.

'If you're keeping him you have to train him properly, Hayley,' said Mum.

'How's she going to do that when she's like a wild animal herself!' said Keira.

'I'll show you,' I said. 'I'm going to train Magpie until he's the most obedient dog in the world. We'll do an act together. We can be on *Britain's Got Talent*!'

Well, I tried. I even went to puppy training classes but I didn't really get on with the teacher.

Now there's a surprise!

She was so bossy. She got on my nerves. And she got on Magpie's nerves too. He didn't want to mess around walking to heel.

25

He likes jumping about and dashing this way and that. He didn't want to lie down and wait. He wanted to run and join me and play with all the other puppies. He didn't want to learn to leave a treat until I said he could have it. He wanted to gobble it up straight away.

I understand your motive, Hayley, but you know perfectly well it's against school rules for anyone to leave the premises at lunchtime!

Magpie and I

I want Magpie to have fun. And we do, big time. I take him for two walks a day, before and after school, and I charge home at lunchtime to make sure he's all right too.

It's especially magic at the weekend because I don't have to go to boring old school. Me and Magpie can stay together all day long and do whatever we like. We go for long walks in heaps of different parks and he goes for a swim in the ponds and chases after all the other dogs and we share crisps for lunch, yum yum.

I have to feed Magpie lots because he's a growing boy. He's much bigger now. And his spots have mostly joined up. I don't think he's really a Dalmatian any more. The man in the pet shop says he's a Licorice Allsorts. I don't care. I love Magpie to bits even if he's not a pedigree.

Sooooo I was really looking forward to the summer holidays at first because it meant I could be with Magpie twenty-four seven. I was planning all sorts of crazy expeditions for him and me. But then Mum and Keira ruined everything!

No such word!

Keira was going on about how boring it was, just staying home for six weeks, and how it wasn't fair because all her mates were going abroad and why couldn't we. She went on and on and on about it, until Mum had a rush of blood to the head and went on the internet when Keira and I went to bed.

Mum woke us in the morning looking triumphant.

'Guess what, girls! We're going on holiday after all! I found a brilliant last minute deal – we're having eight days

🐚 27 🐚

in Benidorm, how about that? Lots of sun and lots of fun!'

'Oh wow, Mum, thanks a million!' Keira squealed.

'Cool, eh?' said S.S.

'No, it'll be hot. Too hot!' I said. 'Dogs don't like the heat. And the only way they can cool down is to pant. Poor Magpie is going to spend the entire holiday with his tongue hanging out.'

'Don't be silly, Hayley! Magpie can't come on holiday with us! We're staying in a fancy hotel. They'd never let Magpie come in a million years. Besides, how on earth would he cope with a plane journey? We're obviously leaving him at home,' said Mum.

'Then I'm staying at home too!' I declared.

Then there was an argument. It went on for a long time. Mum said Magpie had to go into kennels for a week.

'No way!' I insisted. 'It would be like putting him in prison. He'd absolutely hate it. He'd be so worried without me. He'd think he'd been abandoned again. No, this isn't going to happen. You

lot can all go to Benidorm but Magpie and me are staying at home.'

There was a LOT of argument then. I won't bore you writing it all out but it was mega mega mega.

I can imagine.

Mum and S.S. made it clear that they'd snatch Magpie and lock him up in these awful kennels and frog-march me to the airport no matter how I screamed and kicked. I was horribly scared they might be right. So I devised a CUNNING PLAN!!!!!!!

We were due to leave on an evening flight on Friday, taking my poor Magpie to doggy-jail on the way. So on the Thursday I suddenly stopped protesting bitterly and acted all sorry and goody goody and went and packed a suitcase with my favourite T-shirts and jeans and shorts and my toy teddy that always sleeps with me and don't you dare laugh. I also packed a carrier bag for Magpie with all his special stuff too: his doggy treats and chewy things and his spare lead and his favourite ball and his squeaky toy and his little red blanket and his totally revolting cow's ear.

Unnecessary capital letters and too many exclamation marks again. Though I must admit I'm on tenterhooks wanting to discover your cunning plan, Hayley.

'Good girl, Hayley,' said Mum. 'I'm glad you've seen sense at last.'

Unpleasant word

Again, so is only a two-letter word.

I hope it's not what I think it is!

I think there are multiple problems, Hayley!

HAYLEY!

I wasn't being good. I was being very bad. I had no intention of going on a poxy holiday and putting my pooch in those rubbish kennels. Magpie would be shut up most of the time and he'd soooooo hate that.

I bet you can't guess my CUNNING PLAN!

I was going to run away! I planned to get up ever so early and creep out of the house with Magpie and our luggage and then off we'd trot. I wasn't exactly sure where we would run to. I had a vague idea that we'd hop on a train and maybe make for our own British seaside so Magpie and I could have a bit of a holiday too. We could play on the beach all day and go swimming and eat fish and chips and ice cream and sleep under the pier at night.

It was a brilliant plan. There was just one slight problem.

I didn't have any spare cash. So when I got up very early in the morning on Friday I borrowed a little bit from S.S.'s wallet.

It wasn't much. He'd already changed a lot of it into euros to use as holiday money. I just used the rest. He wouldn't be needing it, would he, not if he was away in Spain.

So, Magpie and I had some spare cash so we were all set. We decided to make ourselves scarce as soon as possible. So I helped myself to Mum's mobile and set the alarm thingy ever so ever so early and hid it under my pillow. I didn't really need it, actually, because I was so keyed up I hardly slept all night, and I was wide awake by six in the morning. So I whispered in Magpie's ear that he had to be quiet as a mouse and he licked my face all over and assured me I didn't need to worry.

HAYLEY!

I shoved on some clothes quick, tiptoed to the bathroom and back, picked up our bags, and then we crept to the front door and let ourselves out. Mum and S.S. and Keira stayed sound asleep, snoring their little heads off. It was easy-peasy!

I very much hope you're making all this up to tease me, Hayley! Do you have any idea how dangerous this could be?

I wasn't the slightest bit scared. Magpie and I set off down the road together. Magpie couldn't believe his luck that he was going for walkies so early in the day. He darted about on the end of his lead, smelling the pavement excitedly and stopping to do a wee on almost every lamp post we passed.

We called in at the corner shop as we hadn't had any breakfast yet, so we shared a packet of crisps. I was a bit loaded with our bags and everything so we sat at the edge of the kerb and had a good munch. I wasn't exactly sure how to get to the railway station but I was sure we'd find it easily enough.

'We're having a great time, aren't we, Magpie?' I said, letting him lick out the crisp bag, and he wagged his tail happily in agreement.

It was all going so well – but then along comes this dirty great police car, and when the driver saw us he drew up and parked beside us. I felt like scarpering as soon as possible, but I didn't want to make the police guy suspicious and I knew I wouldn't be able to make Magpie run with me, not while he had his head in a crisp bag.

'Hi there,' said the policeman, sticking

32

his head out of the car window. 'You're early birds, you and your dog.'

'Yeah, well, we've got places to go, trains to catch,' I said airily, looking him straight in the eye to stop him being suspicious.

'Are you all on your ownio?' asked the policeman.

'No,' I said. 'I'm with Magpie here.'

'Ah! Hello there, Magpie.' The policeman got out of his car. 'He's a fine looking fellow, isn't he?'

I warmed to him then, even if he was a nosy old copper.

'He looks like he's finished his crisps now. Do you think he might fancy a sausage sandwich? My missus always gives me a packed lunch when I'm on early turn.' He rummaged back inside the car and unpeeled some tinfoil. Magpie's head jerked upwards and he started drooling. Sausages are his all time favourite food, but my mum won't cook us bangers and mash any more because Magpie goes berserk and wants to scoff the lot.

You frequently try this approach with me, Hayley, but it doesn't work!

He leaped up at the policeman now. He chuckled and gave him half a sandwich. Magpie wolfed it down and whined hopefully for the other half. I couldn't blame him. It did look very tempting. The crisps had acted as an appetizer and now I was starving.

'Come on, kid, get in the car and you can stuff yourselves all you want,' he said, opening the door for me.

'I wasn't born yesterday,' I said. 'As if I'd get in a car with a strange man!'

'Yep, very wise,' he said. 'So I'll introduce myself. I'm P.C. Hargreaves. Look. Here's my warrant card. And if you'd like to radio in to the station they'll confirm I'm a genuine copper.'

I'd always fancied trying out a police radio and talking in all that delta foxtrot lingo – but I didn't dare risk it. Mum might have phoned the police already after searching the house high and low. They'd keep me talking and give P.C. Hargreaves some secret tip off and then he'd arrest me and Magpie.

'I'll believe you,' I said. I picked up Magpie and our bags and we slid into the car. 'Bring on the breakfast!'

But quick as a wink he'd locked the doors,
trapping us.

'You pig! You tricked us!' I said furiously.

'Yes. Afraid I have,' said P.C. Hargreaves.
'I'm going to take you back to your home,
wherever it is, because it's clear to me that
you two are runaways.'

'You mean fibbing whatsit!' I said.

'I might be mean but I'm not fibbing
about the sausage sandwiches. Tuck in
while you tell me all about it.'

He offered me the packet of sandwiches.
I wasn't going to have any but Magpie
snuffled one up straight away, so I helped
myself too.

'Have you had a row with Mum?' he asked.

'Yep,' I said with my mouth full. 'And my
stupid stepdad.'

'So what was it about? Did they tell you
off about something?' He paused. 'Are they
really mean to you, kid?'

Hayley!
You called
a policeman
a pig?

'Yes!' I said. 'They're trying to make me go to Benidorm!'

He burst out laughing.

'Ooh, very very mean of them!' he said. 'I think we'd better take you into care straight away!'

'I don't mind. That would be fine, so long as I can take Magpie too,' I said, though I knew he was joking.

'So what's so terrible about Benidorm?' he said. 'My mum and dad go there every summer. They love it there. Sand, sun, lovely swimming pools.'

'But they won't let me take Magpie! They say he's got to go into kennels and he'd hate hate hate it there, all locked up. It would be just like prison for him,' I wailed, getting so worked up my sandwich went down the wrong way and I choked.

'There, there,' said P.C. Hargreaves, patting me on the back. 'Choke up, chicken. Kennels aren't all bad, you know.'

'I bet you tell all the criminals you arrest that prisons aren't all bad,' I said.

This made him laugh again.

'You're a caution, you are – you and your cute mutt,' he said, patting Magpie.

Magpie felt flattered and jumped off my lap onto P.C. Hargreaves' knee and did his big-brown-eyes-please-love-me expression.

'Oh, yes, you're a great little guy,' said P.C. Hargreaves.

Magpie nodded in agreement and tucked himself under his arm.

'How does he get on with other dogs?' he asked.

'He loves them.'

'And little kids?'

'He loves them too. He loves everyone.'

'And when are you supposed to go to Benidorm?'

'This evening.'

'My goodness! Well, we'd better get you home, pronto. And I'll meet your mum and stepdad, right? And then maybe – just maybe, mind – I could look after Magpie here while you're on your hols. My missus and I have got two dogs of our own, Labradors called Sunny and Bingo. She works part time to fit in with taking the kids to school, and I collect them and look after the whole caboodle in the afternoon. So I dare-say we could look after Magpie too. In our home, which is definitely not like a kennel.'

'Oh, P.C. Hargreaves!' I threw myself at him and gave him such a grateful hug that I knocked his police hat off, which is probably a serious offence but he didn't charge me, thank goodness.

He took me home and DO YOU KNOW WHAT?????

Unnecessary capitals and too many question marks. But never mind, I'm dying to know if everything worked out all right!

When we got home the curtains were still drawn and Mum and S.S. and Keira were all still fast asleep in bed! Shows how much they cared about me! I'd been gone for ages and ages and ages and yet there they were, snoring away. Mum just about died when she came to the front door in her nightie, her hair all over the place, and saw me and Magpie and P.C. Hargreaves.

There was a lot of telling off. 'Hayley, how could you!' Blah-blah-blah – but after P.C. Hargreaves had come inside and had a cup of tea it was all decided. He really was happy to look after Magpie until we got back from Benidorm. I knew Magpie would still miss me dreadfully but I was certain he'd get on fine with P.C. Hargreaves and his missus and his kids and he'd especially like to be with Sunny and Bingo.

So that was that. And I went to Benidorm with Mum and S.S. and Keira. And it was OK. Sunny and sandy, like he said. And our hotel had an ace swimming pool. I was still worried about Magpie missing me, but P.C. Hargreaves texted to Mum's mobile nearly every day, and he sent photos of Magpie romping with Sunny and Bingo to put my mind at rest.

All sorts happened on holiday (like Keira got her first boyfriend and stayed out late and for once she was the one in big trouble, not me!) but I've done you hundreds of pages already, Mrs Spencer, and Mum says I have to go to bed now and Magpie needs one last walk or he'll do a wee on the carpet. Sooooooo – that was my summer holiday. I bet I've written more than anyone else.

You have indeed, Hayley. I've enjoyed your essay enormously. Your writing style is much too colloquial – but you certainly know how to spin a story. Well done! 10/10 and a gold star!!!!! (For once I think several exclamation marks are required.)

☆ DID YOU KNOW . . . ? ☆

• The first day of summer is called the summer solstice. Solstice is Latin for 'sun stand still'. The sun is higher in the sky throughout the day, and its rays beam on the Earth at a more direct angle, causing hotter temperatures.

• The names of the summer months come from the Ancient Romans! June is named after Juno, the wife of Jupiter, the king of the Roman gods. July is named after the famous Roman Emperor Julius Caesar, and August after his nephew, Augustus.

• In the summer, the Eiffel Tower in Paris grows by around six inches. The heat makes the metal expand!

• Ice lollies were invented by accident! On a very cold night in 1905, 11-year-old Frank Epperson mixed soda and water, and left the mixture out with the stirring spoon still in it. The mixture froze, creating the first ice lolly – and the spoon became the stick! Ice lollies are called popsicles in America, and icy poles in New Zealand.

- While the summer months in the northern hemisphere are June, July and August, this time of year is actually winter in the southern hemisphere. This means that in Australia, their summer happens while we're celebrating Christmas!

- The term 'the dog days of summer' means the hottest, stickiest days of the year, between the start of July and the middle of August. The name comes from the Dog Star, Sirius, in the constellation of Canis Minor.

- In America, July is National Ice Cream Month!

- One of our most popular fruity summer snacks – watermelon – is actually a vegetable! It belongs to the same family as cucumbers and pumpkins.

BURIED ALIVE!

This is my holiday diary. Whoops. My writing is a bit wobbly because I am in the car. My mum gave Biscuits and me these diaries. There was a red diary and a brown diary. This is the brown one. I really wanted the red but I had to let Biscuits choose first. Biscuits is my best ever friend. I think.

I am going on holiday with my mum and my dad and my friend Biscuits.

WALES

Tim's diary

Biscuits' diary

I had a big breakfast with sausages (yum) because I was going on a long journey.

Then we stopped at the motorway cafe and guess what. I had a second big breakfast. With egg and bacon and baked beans and more sausages (yum again)

I spent some of my holiday money in the shop. I got fudge and toffee and a giant choc bar

TOFFEE

Giant choc bar

And some chocolate biscuits too. In case I get hungry.

☆ CHAPTER ONE ☆

I'd been looking forward to my holiday for ages and ages. We were going to this seaside place in Wales called Llanpistyll. It is a funny name. It's spelled funny too. It's in Wales and lots of Welsh words are peculiar. Dad says it's a super place though. He went there when he was a boy.

'We had such fun, me and my brothers,' said Dad. 'We swam every day and we made a camp and we played French cricket on the beach and we went for long clifftop walks.'

'I don't want to go on any clifftop walks,' said Mum. 'I hate it when people go too near the edge.'

'I won't go too near the edge, Mum,' I said.

I hate heights too. I went abseiling once. I had to. It was an adventure holiday. It was s-o-o-o-o scary.

 45 🐚

'Shame you haven't got any brothers, Tim,' said Dad. 'It won't be such fun for you.'

'We can have fun together,' said Mum. 'What are the shops like at Llanpistyll?'

'Shops?' said Dad. 'I *think* there's one.'

'*One?*' said Mum. 'What sort of shop?'

'I don't know. A general store, I suppose,' said Dad impatiently. 'You don't go to Llanpistyll to go *shopping*.'

'Obviously not,' said Mum. She sighed. 'I like shopping.'

'So do I,' I said.

Dad sighed too. Even more impatiently. 'Boys don't like shopping,' he said. 'I worry about you sometimes, Tim.'

I worry about my dad sometimes too. He doesn't half go on. And on and on.

'We have a lovely time when we go shopping at the Flowerfields centre on Saturdays, don't we, Tim?' said Mum.

'Tim should be having fun with his friends, not hanging round his mum,' said Dad. Then he stopped and snapped his fingers. 'I've had a brilliant idea!'

I twitched. I don't always like my dad's ideas. Particularly when he thinks they're brilliant. But this time *I* thought it a Truly Dazzling idea.

'Let's invite one of Tim's friends to come to Llanpistyll too,' said Dad.

'Oh *yes*!!!' I said.

46

'Oh no!' said Mum. 'I'm not at all sure about looking after someone else's child. And some of those boys in Tim's class at school are a pretty wild bunch.'

'I don't want to invite anyone from school,' I said. 'I want to invite Biscuits!'

'That boy you met on the adventure holiday?' said Mum.

'The boy who was always eating?' said Dad.

'He seemed quite a nice well-behaved sort of boy,' said Mum. 'Better than that Kelly!'

I met this girl Kelly on the adventure holiday too. She's my girlfriend now. I didn't really choose her. She chose me. She keeps writing to me. She puts all these kisses at the end. It's dead embarrassing. But she's OK really. Quite good fun actually. But nowhere *near* as much fun as Biscuits.

So Dad got in touch with Biscuits' dad. And Mum had a long talk on the phone with Biscuits' mum. It was all fixed!

I was thrilled. Biscuits was thrilled.

Kelly was not at all thrilled when I wrote and told her.

She wrote back: 'You mean rotten stinking pig. Why didn't you ask *me* to go to this Llanpissy place with you? Though I'm going to have a MUCH better holiday. My mum's got this new boyfriend with a caravan and we're all going to go camping and it'll be heaps more fun. And I *might* have asked you to come too but I'm not now. So there.'

I got a bit worried I might have upset Kelly.

'But Kelly's just my *girl*friend. Biscuits is my best ever *friend* friend,' I said to Mum. 'I'm so so so pleased he's coming on holiday. We'll have such fun together. We laughed and mucked around and played all these daft games together when we were on that adventure holiday. It was great.'

'I thought you said you'd had a terrible time,' said Mum. 'Oh dear. I think I'd better buy a good book for this holiday.'

She sounded a bit huffy. I got the feeling I'd somehow upset her too.

'It's only natural that Tim wants to play games with his pal. Do you know how to play French cricket, Tim? It's a great game – but you'll need me to join in too, to make up the numbers.'

'Biscuits and me don't like French or cricket, Dad. We play our own games. He's Biscuits-Boy and I'm Super-Tim,' I said.

'Oh. Right. I see,' said Dad. He suddenly sounded huffy too.

I seemed to have upset everyone.

I felt upset myself the morning of the holiday. Truly seriously upset. I felt sick and shaky and my tummy kept squeezing so I couldn't eat my breakfast.

 48

'Oh dear, oh dear, I do hope you're not going down with anything nasty, Tim,' said Mum, feeling my forehead.

'He's fine. He's just tired because it's so early,' said Dad, yawning.

It was *ever* so early, still practically night time. We had to make an early start because Llanpistyll is a very long way.

'We've had to make an even earlier start than usual to pick up Biscuits on the way. You do realize, Tim, it's adding a good fifty miles to the journey,' said Dad.

'Biscuits is such a silly name. I hope he's not a silly boy. I don't want you two messing around too much, Tim. I don't like it when you get over-excited,' said Mum. 'Is that why you're feeling funny, dear? Because you're so looking forward to seeing him?'

I didn't know. I suddenly felt *shy*. I knew I liked Biscuits ever so much. But what if he didn't like me this time? Maybe he'd changed? Maybe he'd think me a bit weird now? And what would he think of my mum and dad?

I'd packed Walter Bear in my suitcase but I had to rush to my bedroom and get him out and have a quick nuzzle into his warm furry head. Then I saw myself in the mirror.

I saw this boy and this bear having a cuddle. Maybe Biscuits would think me a great big *baby*?

 49

'Come *on*, Tim, I thought you'd done all your packing,' said Dad, peering round my door. 'Put that silly bear down and get a move on.'

Dad certainly thought me a great big baby. I don't think he likes Walter Bear one bit.

'Do you *really* have to take that old bear with you?' said Dad.

'Yes, I really have to, Dad,' I said clinging to Walter.

'Well, pack it away, then! You don't want Biscuits to laugh at you, do you?' said Dad, and he snatched Walter and shoved him on top of my folded holiday clothes and slammed the case shut.

'Dad! Watch out! His legs are all twisted back – and his nose will get squashed! He wants me to make him a special nest in my T-shirts,' I wailed.

'Oh give me strength!' said Dad. 'You mind I don't pack *you* in the suitcase too. Now go and get in the car this minute while I lock up the house and get the boot loaded.'

'No, wait! Tim, have you done a last wee?' said Mum.

'Yes!'

'When? I should do another one just in case,' said Mum.

I wondered if Mum would keep asking if I needed to have a wee when Biscuits was around. Maybe Dad was right. Maybe he *would* laugh at me.

It was a very long drive up to where Biscuits lived.

I sat. I looked out the window. I bit my nails.

'Are you all right, Tim? You're ever so quiet,' said Mum. 'You're not feeling sick, are you?'

'A bit,' I said.

'Oh, dear,' said Mum. 'Here, have a barley sugar. Maybe we should have given you a travel pill. Wind the window down a bit, dear. If you really feel you're going to be sick, do try to tell Dad in time, won't you?'

'He's not going to be sick,' said Dad. 'Don't keep on about it. Try to take his mind off it.'

'Well, I've got some little treats in my bag – but I was going to wait until Biscuits could share them too. Why don't you just cuddle up with Walter Bear, Tim?'

'I *can't*. He's shut in the suitcase. With his legs bent back and his nose squashed sideways,' I said mournfully.

'Do give it a rest – both of you!' said Dad.

Mum went into a huff.

I went in a huff too, though I'm not sure Dad noticed.

Then I fell asleep for a bit.

'Wake up, Tim!' Dad called. 'We're nearly at Biscuits' house. Now, according to this map they sent, Marlow Road should be . . . oh blow, we've just gone past it!'

 51

It took another ten minutes of turning down one-way roads and doing U-turns before we eventually arrived outside Biscuits' house. And there was Biscuits on the doorstep.

'There he is! Well, get out the car, Tim, and run and say hello,' said Dad.

'We'll all get out, darling,' said Mum. 'Come on. What's the matter? You're not shy, are you?'

I felt s-o-o-o-o shy I couldn't say a word. Biscuits didn't seem the slightest bit shy.

'Hey, Tim! I've been looking out for you for ages! Hi, Mrs Parsons, Mr Parsons. My mum says do you want to come inside for a cup of tea?'

'It's very kind of you but we'd better get on our way,' said Dad.

All the same, the two mums talked for ten minutes about mealtimes and bedtimes and boring stuff like that, and the two dads talked about motorways and petrol and boring stuff like *that*.

'We could have had a cup of tea after all,' said Biscuits. '*And* biscuits.'

'Are you hungry, dear?' said Mum.

'You bet,' said Biscuits.

'Well, we'll stop at a motorway café quite soon,' said Mum.

'Great,' said Biscuits. He nudged me.

'Great, Tim, yeah?'

'Yeah,' I said. My voice was still all little and whispery.

'Tim's feeling a bit shy,' Mum announced.

I could have kicked her. Everyone looked at me. I went red.

'Do you think you ought to have a quick wee while we're here, Tim?' Mum said. She lowered her voice a bit this time – but everyone still heard. I went redder than ever.

I wouldn't go, even though I quite wanted to. Biscuits said goodbye to his mum and dad and then we got in the car and set off.

'Would you boys like a barley sugar?' said Mum, passing us the bag.

'Yes please,' said Biscuits. He put three in his mouth at once and sucked happily. 'Yum, I'm starving.'

'We'll stop at the first café we come to when we're on the motorway,' Mum said.

Dad wanted to carry on driving but Mum said Biscuits could obviously do with a proper breakfast. So we stopped at the first service station. We made a trip to the toilets first. I had to dash to get there in time. Then we went to the cafeteria. Mum and I just had tea and toast. Dad said he might as well have a fry-up now he was here.

'That sounds a great idea,' said Biscuits. 'Can I have one too? With bacon and lots of sausages? Yum!'

 53

'You've certainly got a healthy appetite, young man,' said Dad.

'I think it's an *un*healthy appetite,' said a funny squeaky voice. Something pink and knitted popped out of Biscuits' pocket.

'It's Dog Hog!' I said. 'I'd forgotten all about him! It's your doggy piggy thing your granny knitted.'

'Yes, I'm Dog Hog. Fancy forgetting me!' Biscuits made Dog Hog say. He pretended to poke me with one of his floppety arms. Then Dog Hog gave Biscuits a poke too. 'You're not to eat bacon or sausages! They might very well be my distant relations.'

'Well, your distant relations taste ever so yummy,' said Biscuits cheerily.

'Horrid greedy boy,' said Dog Hog. Biscuits made Dog Hog's head wobble from side to side.

'What's he looking for?' I said.

'I'm looking for a certain Mr Bear I've heard a lot about,' said Dog Hog.

'Oh, you want to meet Walter Bear!' I said. 'Well, he's all stuffed into my suitcase at the moment, isn't he, Dad?'

Dad sighed – but his big breakfast had put him in a good mood. When we got back in the car he got my suitcase out of the boot and pulled Walter Bear out.

Poor poor Walter Bear. I straightened his legs very

gently. He lay back stiffly in my arms, his entire snout squashed out of shape.

'I don't think he's been able to breathe a bit!' I said, trying to rub his nose back into position.

'Here, let Dog Hog get at him,' said Biscuits, and he made Dog Hog bend over and put his woolly mouth on Walter's.

'What *is* he doing? *Kissing* him?' I said.

'No! He's giving him artificial respiration,' said Biscuits.

'Oh, right,' I said happily. I pummelled Walter Bear's furry chest. 'I'll help too. Come on, Walter, start breathing again.'

I made Walter take a great big breath and sit up.

'Ah! Thank you so much,' I made him say, in a deep growly voice. 'Who is this kind pink person, Tim? He's certainly saved my bacon. Whoops! Pardon the expression.'

'This is Dog Hog, Walter Bear.'

'I like Dog Hog, Tim,' said Walter Bear.

'So do I,' I said.

And I liked Biscuits too. Ever so much. I wasn't shy any more. Not one bit.

'I'm glad you're coming on holiday with us, Biscuits,' I said.

'Me too!' said Biscuits. 'Hey, I'm glad this isn't an adventure holiday like last time.'

'You can say that again!'

'I'm glad this isn't an adventure holiday like last time.'

'You can say that again!'

We both started cracking up laughing. But we were *wrong*.

This holiday was going to be Truly Terribly Adventurous!

Tim's diary

I am here and guess what. Dad is right. LLanpistyll is brilliant. Biscuits and I get the giggles whenever we say LLanpistyll. We say it a lot. HEAPS of things have happened. Biscuits nearly committed a murder.

Eek!

And I built the Eighth Wonder of the World (miniature version) but then it was destroyed by a Deadly Fiendish Enemy.

D.F.E.'s mate

Biscuits' diary

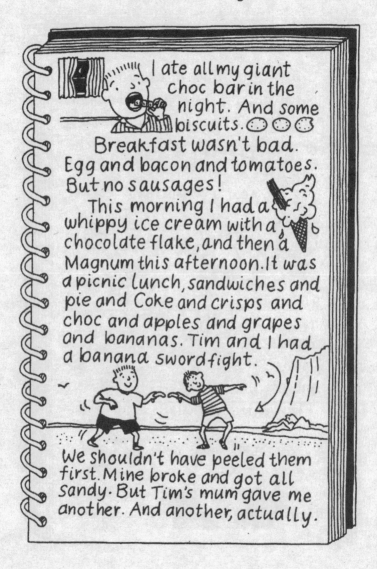

I ate all my giant choc bar in the night. And some biscuits. ◯◯◯

Breakfast wasn't bad. Egg and bacon and tomatoes. But no sausages!

This morning I had a whippy ice cream with a chocolate flake, and then a Magnum this afternoon. It was a picnic lunch, sandwiches and pie and Coke and crisps and choc and apples and grapes and bananas. Tim and I had a banana sword fight.

We shouldn't have peeled them first. Mine broke and got all sandy. But Tim's mum gave me another. And another, actually.

✧ CHAPTER TWO ✧

Our hotel was called the Gwesty Bryn Nodfa.
Gwesty is Welsh for hotel. We were guests in the
Gwesty. There weren't many other guests because it's
quite a little hotel.

Two old ladies looked out of the Gwesty guest
lounge and saw Biscuits and me and said, 'Oh dear!
Boys! They'll start rampaging around in their great
big boots.'

So Biscuits whispered in my ear, 'Oh dear! *Old
ladies!* They'll start rampaging around in their great
big Scholl sandals.'

I cracked up laughing. Biscuits did too. Mum
frowned at us.

'Boys! Calm down now.' She looked apologetically at
the old ladies. 'Don't worry, they're very well-behaved
boys.'

'But I bet they're very badly behaved old ladies,' Biscuits whispered.

I cracked up laughing again. Biscuits did too. We couldn't stop even when Mum got really cross. Biscuits laughed so much he choked on the last bit of a Kit Kat he'd been munching and he had to be patted on the back. Little bits of Kit Kat – Kitten Krumbs – spattered out of his mouth and slurped down his chin.

'Really!' said Mum, whipping out her hankie.

'Oh leave the boys be. It's just high spirits,' said Dad. 'Come on, don't let's bother with unpacking. Let's get on the beach while the sun's still out.'

So we walked to the beach. We loped down all these little lanes with hedges full of honeysuckle and wild roses and harebells. We spotted one hedgehog and two butterflies and three rabbits and four magpies. Mum said it seemed a very long way to this beach.

Then we had to skirt round a cabbage field and Biscuits and I had a long discussion about the general disgustingness of cabbage. Even Biscuits isn't keen on eating something that pongs of old drains. Mum said she was sure we were lost and she was getting a blister.

Then we had to climb over a stile. It was fun sorting out which way to put your legs. Dad said they were also called kissing gates. He helped Mum climb over and when she was balancing at the top he kissed her! I was dead embarrassed. Biscuits and I raised our eyebrows and made smarmy sucky kissing noises. Mum went very pink but she didn't tell us off. Her blister didn't seem to be hurting her any more because she didn't lag behind. She bounced along arm in arm with Dad, while Biscuits and I ran ahead because we could see the sea at last.

'Careful!' Mum shouted. 'Don't go too near the edge, boys!'

But we weren't at the top of a steep chalky cliff. It was all sandy grass and then there was just a long slope of wonderful soft sand in front of us, down down down to the beach.

'Wheeeeeeee!' shouted Biscuits, and he started sliding down on his bottom.

'Wheeeeeeee!' I shouted too, sliding likewise. I had sand all up my T-shirt and shorts but I didn't care a bit. I leaned over sideways and tumbled over and over, shrieking.

'Wow!' said Biscuits, and he turned sideways and started tumbling too.

He looked like a great big beachball bouncing all the way down.

By the time I got to the bottom I had sand in my hair and my ears and my mouth and even up my nose but I still didn't care. I just took off my T-shirt and rubbed it all off. Biscuits did the same.

'Keep your T-shirts *on*, boys. You don't want to get sunburnt!' Mum called.

She rubbed us all over with this sunscreen stuff. It was ever so tickly and Biscuits and I both got the giggles. Then the sun went in and soon we needed our T-shirts back on, *and* our sweaters.

'How about a game of French cricket to get warm?' said Dad.

'Oh Dad. No! I hate games like that,' I said.

'You've never even played it. Come on, it's *fun*, Tim,' said Dad.

'Why don't you all make a nice sandcastle?' said Mum quickly.

'Oh yes!' I said. I know about castles. I did this special project at school. 'Let's build a motte and bailey castle, eh, Biscuits?' I said.

'You what?' said Biscuits. 'Bot and naily?'

'You twit! Motte. That's a castle that's up on a mound, right? And the bailey is the walk right round it.'

'No, don't let's build a boring old motte and bailey castle, Tim. We'll do my bot and naily castle. All the soldiers stand up the top and moon at the enemy showing their bots, right?'

'OK, OK,' I said, giggling. 'And then they cut off all their horny old toenails and flick them over the parapets so that it's like confetti and all these daggy old nailies get in the enemies' hair, right, Biscuits?'

'What on earth are you two going on about?' said Dad, getting a bit irritated. 'OK, let's build a sandcastle.'

There was just one problem. We didn't have any decent spades. There was a little kiosk right along at the top of the beach so we trailed all the way there but they just had little baby plastic spades for toddlers. They had ice-cream though so we had that instead.

I was a bit disappointed. I had this vision of a brilliant turreted castle on a mound with *garderobes* and arrow-slit windows and a little drawbridge. But Biscuits licked his ice-cream happily and didn't seem to mind a bit.

When we went back to the hotel I spotted something in the umbrella stand in the hall. Two big spades with painted wooden handles and hard metal blades. They were very old and chipped but still sturdy. They looked as if they'd been lolling in the umbrella stand a very long time.

The hotel lady, Mrs Jones, made a fuss of Biscuits at dinner because he had mushroom soup and a roll and then chicken and chips and peas and then apple pie and cream and he said it was all extra yummy, especially the pie. Mrs Jones said it was her own special home-made pie and she brought him another slice because she said it was good to see a young man who appreciated his food.

I hadn't been able to finish my pie and I didn't like

the skin on my chicken and I don't like soup, especially not mushroom.

Mum apologized for me being such a picky eater but Mrs Jones just laughed and ruffled my hair. She seemed to like me too even though I don't appreciate my food like Biscuits. So I plucked up courage to ask about the spades.

'Those old spades, dearie? Of course you two boys can borrow them.'

'Wow! Great!' I said.

'Wow and wow again and great and even greater,' said Biscuits.

We went to inspect the spades in the umbrella stand while Mum and Dad had coffee.

'I'll have the one with the red handle,' said Biscuits, grabbing it.

'But you had the red holiday diary,' I said.

'Yes, so red's my colour,' said Biscuits. 'You can have the blue.'

'But I was the one who asked about the spades,' I said. 'And I let you have first pick of the holiday diaries so I should have first pick now.'

'It's only an old *spade*,' said Biscuits, but he hung on to it. He lifted it in the air like a sword. 'I challenge you to a duel, Super-Tim.'

'OK, OK, Biscuits-Boy,' I said, seizing the blue spade reluctantly.

I hoped he was joking. Biscuits seemed a lot stronger than me – and the spades were heavy, with sharp edges.

Biscuits lunged. I dodged. Biscuits went on lunging, slightly off balance – and very nearly speared one of the old ladies shuffling out of the dining room. She shrieked. Her friend shrieked too. Mum came running and she shrieked as well. She couldn't get cross with Biscuits because he was our guest. So she got cross with me. Which wasn't fair. Not one bit.

'Sorry you got the telling off, Tim,' Biscuits said, when we were in our room.

'It's OK,' I said, though I was still feeling ever so miffed.

'Look. You can have the red spade if you really want it,' said Biscuits.

'It's OK,' I repeated, not quite so miffed.

'I insist,' said Biscuits.

'Right! The red spade's mine,' I said, suddenly not miffed at all. I giggled. 'You didn't half make that old lady jump, Biscuits.'

'I nearly skewered her like a kebab,' said Biscuits, and he giggled too.

We mimed the mock duel all over again. We couldn't act it out because we'd been told *very firmly* that the spades had to be kept in the umbrella stand all the time we were in the hotel.

We had a duel with our toothbrushes instead and that was great fun, even though Biscuits kept winning. Then Mum came in to settle us down and she made a bit of a fuss about the frothy toothpaste all over everywhere but she didn't get too narky this time.

'I suppose boys will be boys,' she said. 'Now, it's been a long day and you were up very early, Tim. Time to snuggle down and go to sleep.'

We snuggled down. But of course we didn't go to sleep. We held an amazingly rude competition. Then we had a joke-telling bonanza. Biscuits knows some wonderfully disgusting jokes. I snorted so much I had to bury my head in the pillow. So did Biscuits. And then he realized he'd lain on his night-time emergency pack of biscuits. There were an awful lot of crumbs. He had to eat them all up to get rid of them.

Then he nodded off. Biscuits makes little munching noises even in his sleep. Then I went to sleep too and dreamed I was down on the beach, building the biggest sandcastle in the world. I stepped inside and explored, climbing the narrow steps round and round, right to the top of the golden tower . . .

Then I woke up and it was morning. The first thing I thought of was Castle.

Then Biscuits woke up and the first thing he did was sniff hopefully.

'Hi, Biscuits! Are you seeing if you can smell the sea air?'

'Hi, Tim! No, I'm seeing if I can sniff sausages for breakfast!' said Biscuits.

'No, no, no, Mr Cannibal,' said Dog Hog, struggling out from under the sheets and attacking Biscuits.

Walter Bear and I watched, cuddling peacefully.

'You are crackers, Biscuits,' I said. 'Hey, can I really have the red spade today?'

'Well, I said you could have it yesterday so really it should be my turn today,' said Biscuits.

'But I never got to use it yesterday!' I said indignantly.

'I'll fight you for the spade, right?' said Biscuits, and he picked up his pillow and thumped me with it.

I thumped back with mine.

We were soon bouncing backward and forward on the beds, thumping and bumping, clouting and shouting. Shouting a little too loudly.

'Boys, boys! Stop it at once!' Mum hissed, rushing into our room in her nightie and dressing gown. 'Honestly! What am I going to do with you? It isn't seven o'clock yet and you're already behaving like horrible hooligans. Now get back into bed and try to have another little snooze.'

We didn't feel the least bit sleepy. We had another weeny-teeny pillow fight, and Biscuits called me a

 67

horrible hooligan and I called Biscuits a horrible hooligan. Then we did a horrible hooligan dance, swaying our hips to be hula-hula hooligans, and Biscuits swayed so much his pyjamas fell down round his ankles. I laughed so hard I fell over in a heap on my bed. Mum came in, Mega-Mad, saying we were waking up all the other guests in the Gwesty and there would be Complaints at Breakfast.

But no one did complain, though the old lady Biscuits had practically skewered flinched nervously as he thundered past her table. Mum was still a bit narky but Dad cheered her up by suggesting we drive to the nearest small town and buy some picnic food and maybe have a little look round the shops.

'Oh n-o-o-o-o-o-o. Biscuits and I want to go straight on the beach with our spades,' I wailed.

But Biscuits seemed to think picnic food might be a seriously good idea, so I didn't make too much fuss. We went to a town called Abercoch. Another name that gave Biscuits and me the giggles. Dad went on about how big it had become and moaned like anything about the amusement arcades and caravan sites and the supermarket in the town centre.

Mum went on about how small it was and why didn't it have a Marks & Spencer and weren't there any decent clothes shops at all? But after we'd got the food we all had an ice-cream and then we got back in the car and parked it at the Gwesty Bryn Nodfa and collected all our beach stuff (including the spades) and walked along the footpaths and around the fields and over the stile and ran all the way down the sandy slope and AT LAST we were on the beach.

I was all set to build the best castle in the world. But guess what. The tide was in. Right in, so that the water was way up, lapping the skirts of the sandy slope. There was barely room to put down our towels and picnic.

'Oh *rats rats rats*,' I said. 'I want to build my castle!'

'Don't say "rats" like that, dear. Now, never mind. You can sit down quietly with Biscuits and read your comics or do some writing in your holiday diaries,' said Mum.

'Never mind, Tim, we can all go for a swim,' said Dad.

'Never mind, Tim, we can maybe have our picnic now instead,' said Biscuits.

'But I wanted to build my *castle*.'

I tried digging in the soft powdery sand of the slope but it was useless. It just slithered and slopped around and wouldn't stand firm at all.

'It's not *fair*.'

'Oh Tim, don't be such a baby,' said Dad. 'Stop making such a fuss about a silly sandcastle. Let's go for a swim.'

 69

'Are you sure the sea is clean enough? You hear such horrible tales about pollution nowadays,' said Mum.

'It's clear as crystal. You come in too,' said Dad.

'Somebody's got to sit here and mind all the picnic things,' said Mum.

'I'll do that,' said Biscuits. He wasn't all that keen on swimming either. But Dad practically pulled us in.

It was f-r-e-e-z-i-n-g. Biscuits and I stood shivering, hugging our elbows, knees knocking, feet solid ice.

'Come on, you two, get in properly,' Dad yelled. 'It's lovely once you're under.' His teeth were chattering too, and his face was purple.

'This isn't my idea of fun,' said Biscuits.

'You can say that again,' I said.

'This isn't my idea of fun,' said Biscuits.

'You can say that— aaaah!' I yelled, because Dad suddenly splashed me.

I splashed him back. And Biscuits. They both splashed each other. And me. Suddenly we were all jumping about and it wasn't quite so cold. It was almost fun.

It was freezing again afterwards, on the beach getting dry, but then we had our picnic and this was very *much* Biscuits' idea of fun – and mine too.

Afterwards Mum lay back and had a little sunbathe. Dad did too. They both started snoring gently, little smiles under their sunhats.

 70

'Let's build our castle!' I said joyfully, because the tide had gone out far enough now and had left gleaming wet wondrous sand just waiting for us to build the best sandcastle in the world.

So we set to, Biscuits and me. I pretty soon realized it wasn't going to be as easy-peasy as I'd thought, even with good sand and sharp spades.

'It's a bit too much like hard work,' Biscuits panted, leaning on his spade. 'Shall we have a sunbathe too, Tim?'

'No, let's make the castle, *please*. Look, you gather shells and seaweed and stuff for decoration if you want a bit of a rest. I'll carry on,' I said nobly.

I carried on. And on and on. I thought of my vision of a castle bigger than me. Now I wondered about a medium-size castle. Or even a small one. I'd only managed a very small mound, so I decided to go for miniature perfection instead of massive bulk.

I squatted down beside my castle and tried to mould it into shape. It was far more finicky than I'd thought. Sand got right up my nails and invaded the legs of my shorts. Little gritty bits embedded themselves in my knees. I tried to fashion a little drawbridge but it was hopeless. My arrow-slit windows weren't exact enough. The tower kept wobbling and collapsing.

'That'll do,' said Biscuits. 'Here, we'll stick little shells in front to make a path, right?'

 71

'You don't have a *path*. We could make a moat. And fill it with water from the sea.'

'Oh-oh,' said Biscuits. 'Something tells me that sounds like hard work.'

We didn't have a bucket so we had to make do with old paper cups. We ran to the sea and filled them up and ran back to the castle and tipped the water in the proposed moat. It immediately disappeared down through the sand.

'Rats,' I said again. I stared at my lop-sided little castle with its empty moat and sighed.

'It's not much of a castle, is it, Biscuits?'

'I think it's a super castle,' said Biscuits. 'Truly. A fantastic creation. Practically the Eighth Wonder of the World. Honest, Tim.'

'Ooooh! Let's see this super-duper castle, eh?' said a loud voice behind us, making us both jump.

Two boys had crept up behind us. One was about our age and very pale and pinched looking. He didn't look very tough but his smile was spiteful. He was the sort of boy you treated with caution.

The other boy was much bigger. And much tougher too. His hair was shaved so short it was just prickles, which looked as sharp as spikes. If he head-butted you you'd get severely perforated. He was the sort of boy that made Red Alert Alarm system, buzz inside your brain.

He was wearing great big Doc Martens even on the beach. I looked at the boy. I looked at the boots. I knew what was going to happen next.

'What a dinky ducky castle you two little cissy boys have made,' he said, his eyes beady. 'Shame it's just sand. Someone could accidentally trip and . . .'

He kicked hard. The castle collapsed. He laughed. His mate laughed.

'You! You big bully! I saw that! You kicked my Tim's castle over deliberately!'

Oh no. It was Mum. She came rushing towards us, red in the face, her dress still tucked up to get her legs suntanned.

The boys spluttered with laughter.

'Mummy's boys!' said the big prickly kicker. 'Don't worry. We'll be back.'

They ran off, laughing and laughing. Biscuits and I didn't laugh at all.

Prickle-Head and Pinch-Face were going to get us!

Tim's diary

I seem to be in the middle of a Dire and Dangerous Adventure.

The Deadly Fiendish Enemy has made another Evil Advance.

Biscuits-Boy and I are desperately outnumbered. (Well, I know it's two against two. But, they're much bigger. Especially Prickle-Head).

However! We have a new recruit to our ranks.

You will never guess who it is.

Biscuits' diary

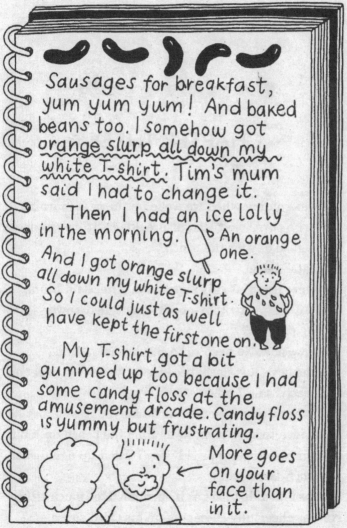

Sausages for breakfast, yum yum yum! And baked beans too. I somehow got orange slurp all down my white T-shirt. Tim's mum said I had to change it.

Then I had an ice lolly in the morning. An orange one.

And I got orange slurp all down my white T-shirt. So I could just as well have kept the first one on.

My T-shirt got a bit gummed up too because I had some candy floss at the amusement arcade. Candy floss is yummy but frustrating.

More goes on your face than in it.

✫ CHAPTER THREE ✫

It was raining when we woke up the next morning. 'Sorry, boys,' said Dad at breakfast. 'It doesn't look like a good day for the beach.'

'Rats!' I said.

'Don't use that silly expression, Tim,' said Mum.

'OK. Large twitchy-nosed long-tailed sewer-scavenging rodents!'

'Now, now. No need to be cheeky,' said Mum.

'The boy's just upset because he was dying to get on the beach,' said Dad.

I wasn't *that* upset, actually. Maybe it wouldn't be a bad idea to keep right away from the beach for a bit. Just in case the big prickly boy turned up again with his pinch-faced pal.

Biscuits didn't look as if he minded too much either. He was cheerfully chomping up his third sausage.

'We'll go for a little drive, eh?' said Dad.

'Yes, let's see if we can find a proper shopping centre,' said Mum.

'I was thinking of a scenic country tour,' said Dad.

Mum sighed. So we toured the country. And it was very scenic. And very wet. We saw grey sky and grey mountains and grey sea.

Biscuits and I got fed up being in the car. But then we saw some people walking in the wet, mud all up their legs. They were huddled under their anorak hoods, water dripping down their noses. Maybe it wasn't so bad in the car after all.

We played I Spy. Dad chose C for Car and Mum guessed it.

Mum chose C for Church and Biscuits guessed it.

Biscuits chose C for Café and I guessed it. So I wanted to choose a C too, but I couldn't think of one. Then I saw something way in the distance, at the top of a mound. Something I'd studied, though I'd never seen one in real life before. Something that had been standing, grey in the gloom but golden in the sunlight, for hundreds and hundreds of years.

'I've got one! I spy with my little eye, something beginning with C!'

Dad guessed Clock (inside the car) and Mum guessed Cardigan (on her) and Biscuits guessed Cabbages (in a pongy old field) and I told them to hurry up a bit or

 77

we'd be way past it, but Dad turned off right and it was still in sight. We were actually going *towards* my C. When Mum and Dad kept guessing silly things they couldn't possibly see like camels and computers and candlesticks I knew that *they* knew and we were going to look round my special C.

Biscuits still didn't get it.

'Cake?' he said hopefully.

'What about C for Chocolate?' said Mum, reaching into her handbag and bringing out a big bar of Cadbury's Dairy Milk. 'Biscuits?'

'Wow, thank you!' said Biscuits, thinking he was getting the whole bar to himself.

'No, dear! Just take a couple of pieces and then pass the bar to Tim. You couldn't possibly eat a whole big bar yourself,' said Mum.

'I could,' said Biscuits. 'Bigger bars than this. Easy peasy.'

'Biscuits' eating powers are phe-nom-en-al,' I said. 'Hey Biscuits, guess my C, go on.'

'Cadbury's!' said Biscuits.

'Your eating powers might be phenomenal, but you're totally *useless* at I Spy,' I said, elbowing him in his big soft side.

'Hey, your skinny little elbows aren't half sharp,' said Biscuits, elbowing me back.

'Hey, your great galumping elbows aren't half

hard,' I said, shoving him.

He shoved back and we started a Mega-Wrestle in the back of the car.

'Boys! Boys! Stop fighting!' Mum shouted.

'They're only messing about,' said Dad.

'They'll choke on their chocolate,' said Mum.

'Anyway, we're here now,' said Dad, pulling up.

'Here! At my special C word!' I said.

'Could it possibly be a Crumbling Creaky *Castle*?' Biscuits laughed, and had another big bite of the chocolate bar when Mum wasn't watching.

He winked at me and I winked at him. Then he winked the other eye and I winked my other eye. Then he winked both rapidly so I did too.

'Tim? Have you got something in your eye, dear? Come here and let me have a look,' said Mum.

'It's nothing, Mum. Don't keep *fussing*,' I said, getting out the car.

'This awful rain,' said Mum. 'You'd better both come under my umbrella, boys.'

'Oh Mum, it's only little drops of water,' I said impatiently. 'Come on, Biscuits-Boy, race you to the top of the tower!'

'Now slow down, Tim. You're not to rush off up anywhere. Old castles can be very dangerous,' said Mum. 'Especially when it's all slippery in the wet. *Tim!*'

'Don't worry, *I'm* not rushing,' said Biscuits.

It took him *ages* and *ages* to get right to the top of the tower. He had to have lots of rests. So did Mum. And even Dad got a bit puffed.

I got to the top FIRST. I've never ever won a proper race before. I'm hopeless going along the ground. I nearly always come last. But I can fly upwards like a rocket. I spread my arms when I was all alone at the top. I stared straight up at the sky, rain pattering on my hot face. I pretended I was really Super-Tim and I'd just whizzed my way over the mountains quick as a wink and now I was waiting to meet up with my trusty companion Biscuits-Boy. Waiting and waiting and waiting.

Biscuits had to sit down when he got to the top. His face was purple.

'Are you all right, Biscuits?' I asked.

He couldn't catch his breath to speak. He shook his head instead.

'Why don't you have a biscuit to make you feel better?' I suggested.

'Don't be silly, Tim, the poor boy might choke,' said Mum.

'A – little – piece – of – choco – late – might – help,' Biscuits wheezed.

'I really don't think you ought to eat quite so much chocolate, dear,' said Mum. 'It's really not very good for you. Hasn't your mother tried to put you on a diet?'

Biscuits' eyes popped in horror.

'My – mum – says – I – need – to – eat – lots – to – keep – my – strength – up!' he gasped.

'Yes, dear, but it's being so heavy that makes you so out of breath,' said Mum.

'Now, now, leave the lad alone. It's not really any of our business,' said Dad. 'Come and look at this fantastic view.'

'I don't want to go too near the edge, it makes me feel so dizzy,' said Mum. 'Don't you go near the edge either, boys.'

I didn't want to go right to the edge of the parapet. I didn't mind at all looking *up* but I knew exactly what it would feel like looking *down*. I went a bit wobbly just thinking about it.

'It's – perfectly – safe,' said Biscuits, his voice stronger now. He pulled a face at my mum's back. I hesitated. Then I pulled one too. We both giggled.

'She doesn't half flap, your mum,' Biscuits whispered.

'Yes, I know. Flap, flap, flap,' I said.

It felt such *fun* to whisper about my mum – but my heart had started to thump.

Biscuits raised his big arms and flapped them. I flapped mine too.

Mum turned round, hanging on to Dad.

'What are you two up to?' she called, looking at our rotating arms.

 81

'We're just pretending to fly, Mum, that's all,' I said quickly.

'Come on, let's peer over,' said Biscuits.

'I don't want to,' I said.

'Look, *I* didn't want to clamber up all those millions and millions of steps so that I practically had a heart attack. But I did. Because you wanted to climb the castle. It's stupid to get right up here and then not even look out. Come on. I want to. So it's only fair that you come too.'

I didn't want to let him down. I knew he was still miffed at my mum. I didn't want him to be miffed at me too. So I took his great plump paw and let him drag me towards the edge of the parapet. It came up to my chin but when I glimpsed the ground far below, the crumbling bricks seemed only ankle height. One small step and I'd be walking into thin air, tumbling down down down to the distant grey slabs below.

I gave a little gasp and shut my eyes tight.

'Wow!' said Biscuits. 'You can see for Mega-Miles, even in the rain. OK, so there's the sea. Which little bay is Llanpistyll? And what about Abercoch? Is it that way – or that?'

'I'm not sure,' I mumbled, pretending to be peering. I had my hands up near my closed eyes so Biscuits wouldn't suss anything.

'And can you see that *other* castle? It's huge! It's got

two towers! And a proper drawbridge and a real moat!' said Biscuits.

'Where?' I said, opening my eyes. I held on to the edge of the parapet so hard my knuckles nearly sprang straight out of my skin. 'I can't see any castle!'

'Funny! Neither can I, now,' said Biscuits, grinning. 'Must have been a mirage. Still – got you looking, didn't it?'

I stuck my tongue out at him. It wasn't quite so scary now that I was getting used to looking. I liked seeing all the wiggly wavy edges of the coast, just like the maps you do at school. It was weird having an eagle-eye view of the world. I stared at the mustard and cress forests, the saucer-size lake, the pencil spire of the tiny toy church, the little matchbox caravan sites until my eyes watered.

I started to enjoy looking across.

I still wasn't so keen on looking directly *down*. But old Biscuits was leaning right *over*.

'Careful, Biscuits!' I said, grabbing him.

'I'm OK. Don't you start flapping now. Here, what's that jutting out bit with the hole? Is that where they poured boiling oil on the invading army?'

I bent my head, my blood pounding. I saw what Biscuits was looking at and laughed wildly.

'No, but it would work almost as well! That's their toilet! They'd do it and it would splash right down so if you were walking about underneath it could land right on your head.'

'*Yuck!*'

We started miming the whole process.

'What on earth are you two boys up to now?' Mum called. 'Why are you rubbing your hair like that, Tim?'

'Oh, I'm just getting a bit wet, that's all,' I said.

'Well, let's go back down and get in the car,' said Mum. 'I wonder if there are any toilets nearby? Tim? Biscuits? What are you two boys laughing at now?'

We found the public toilets – modern version – and then got back in the car and did another little scenic tour. Biscuits casually mentioned chocolate once or twice but Mum said it was too near lunchtime.

We drove to Abercoch. It was only drizzling now so we walked along the seafront and had fish and chips out of a packet, all of us sitting on the wet wall. Mum made us put newspaper down first so that we wouldn't get piles. That made us remember this seriously awful sneery-jeery show-off at the adventure holiday place called Giles – only Biscuits called him Piles.

Mum and Dad had take-away cups of tea and we had ice lollies, and then we went for a walk towards the old broken-down pier.

There was a white wooden kiosk near the entrance with all sorts of painted magic symbols round the door and a sign that said GYPSY ROSE, FORTUNE-TELLER TO THE STARS.

'Ooh look,' said Mum. 'I've always wanted to have my fortune told.'

'Don't be so wet,' said Dad. 'It's all a complete con.'

'No, it's not,' said Mum. 'You don't know anything about it. Tim, shall I have my fortune told?'

'Ooh yes, Mum! Can I have my fortune done too?'

'No dear, it's only for grown-ups.'

'You don't want to waste your money,' said Dad.

'Yes I do,' said Mum.

'She'll just tell you some old rubbish about a romantic encounter with a handsome stranger,' said Dad.

'That sounds good to me,' said Mum, knocking at the little wooden door. 'Keep an eye on the boys while I'm in here.'

'Oh, Mum, can't we come and watch?' I said.

But we had to trail after Dad onto the pier. I hung back.

'What's up, Tim?' said Biscuits. 'Look, *I'll* tell your fortune if you like.' He pulled his T-shirt off and tied it round his head like a gypsy scarf. 'Give me your hand, young man. Aah, what's this I see? An encounter with an *ugly* stranger – one with prickly hair and big boots!'

'I hope not!' I said, snatching my hand away – even though I knew he was just larking around.

 85

'Come *on*, you two,' Dad called to us. 'Biscuits, put your T-shirt on, it's hardly sunbathing weather. And what's up with you, Tim?'

'I don't like the pier,' I mumbled.

'What?' said Dad. 'What are you on about? Let's go and see if the lads fishing have caught anything.'

'I don't think much of this pier either,' Biscuits said. 'It's all old and boring. Only one ice-cream stall. They haven't got any doughnuts or rock or burger bars.'

'Yes, rotten old pier,' I said, though I didn't care about the lack of food stalls.

I didn't like the pier itself. I worried about the way the wooden planks were seldom perfectly slotted together. You could see through the gaps down to the frothy grey sea underneath. Some of the planks looked really old, as if they'd splinter as soon as you stepped on them.

I tried to work out the width of the plank and the width of me. It was fine for someone big like Biscuits. But I'm seriously skinny. I could quite possibly go plummeting downwards to my death. Well, I can swim a bit so maybe I wouldn't drown immediately. But I knew there are all sorts of dangerous currents under piers. Even very strong swimmers could be sucked straight under.

'Why are you walking in that funny way?' asked Biscuits.

 86

'Oh, I – I'm just playing that don't-step-on-the-cracks-game,' I said quickly.

I didn't want to tell Biscuits I was scared of the pier. He'd start to think me the wimpiest wimp ever. He already knew I was scared of heights. And the boy with the prickly hair. (Well, we were *both* a bit scared of him.)

Dad had hurried over to the boys fishing. Biscuits followed. I sidled over, stepping high, holding my breath.

'Maybe we could try a bit of fishing, boys,' Dad said eagerly.

'Yeah, maybe,' said Biscuits. 'Fishing is the sort of sport I like best. You don't rush about. You just sit. And you can eat your fish after!'

I wasn't so sure. I didn't like the idea of being on the pier for ages, especially not perched right at the edge, by the railings.

One of the boys stiffened and hauled in his line.

'He's got one! A real whopper!' said Dad. We edged nearer to watch. It was a big mistake. A great gasping wriggling pop-eyed fish flapped in the air as it was reeled in. The boy seized it and tore the bait from its mouth, ripping it horribly.

'Oh!' I whispered, covering my own lips.

It got a lot worse. The fish was flopping about frantically, its poor torn mouth an O of agony.

 87

The boy held on hard and took aim. I thought he had taken pity on the fish and was going to throw it into the sea. No. He took the gasping fish and whacked its head hard on the wooden planks. The fish stopped flapping. It lay still, a grey slimy sad dead thing.

I felt the fish I'd eaten for lunch flapping inside my tummy. There was a Gents near the end of the pier. I made a run for it, forgetting about the creaking planks in this new emergency. I made it into a cubicle – just. I was very very sick. It was horrible – but it made me feel better too. I didn't want any fish inside me ever again.

Biscuits was waiting for me when I came out.

'Have you been sick?' he asked rather unnecessarily.

'Mmm,' I said, and rinsed my mouth out.

'I'm hardly ever sick,' said Biscuits. 'You must feel horribly empty now. Would you like a biscuit?' He felt in his pocket.

'No thanks!' I said quickly.

'Come and get a bit of fresh air. It's all pongy in here,' said Biscuits.

I must have looked as grey as the poor fish because Biscuits put his arm round me.

'You'll feel better in a minute,' he said, very kindly.

Then we heard a horrible noise from the very end of the pier. Jeering. And then silly juicy kissy noises.

'Ooh! Look at the little Mummy's boys have a cuddle-wuddle!'

It was Prickle-Head and Pinch-Face, sitting up on the railing at the end of the pier, right beside a sign saying DANGER. The sign was Dead Accurate.

Biscuits sprang away from me as if I was red hot. I certainly felt fiery, blood bubbling in my head like a jacuzzi.

'Let's go, Biscuits,' I said urgently, starting to back away.

'Biscuits! What sort of a daft poncey name is that?' said Prickle-Head.

'It's a nickname, right?' said Biscuits. He added, bravely but unwisely, 'Yours is a lot dafter.'

'So what's *my* nickname, eh?' said Prickle-Head, jumping off the railing and standing in front of Biscuits. Pinch-Face copied him, hands on hips, legs wide apart.

I looked round desperately. Dad was still halfway down the pier, talking to the fishermen.

'Looking for Mumsie-Wumsie to come rushing to the rescue?' said Prickle-Head.

'Ooooh dear. She's not around this time, is she? *Shame!* So, Fatso Big-Bum Biscuits – what's *my* nickname, eh?'

Biscuits opened his mouth. I knew he was going to come straight out with it. Prickle-Head. Prickle-Head

 89

would not be amused. He had his great Doc Martens on. Biscuits was as round as a football. It looked like he was going to get kicked.

'Your nickname's The Boss,' I blurted out. Biscuits blinked, astonished.

Prickle-Head looked surprised too.

'The Boss?' he repeated slowly, seeking out hidden insulting meanings.

'Yes, we call you The Boss because you're obviously boss of all the beach,' I said.

Prickle-Head sniggered, obviously dead chuffed with his new nickname.

'OK, OK, so I'm The Boss,' he said. 'Check that out, Ricky.'

'Right, Carl,' said Pinch-Face.

'Right, *Boss*,' said Prickle-Head. Then he turned to me. 'What's your nickname then, if your tubby pal is Biscuits? Are you Little Squirt?'

Pinch-Face snorted.

'Yes!' I said. 'Yes, that's me. I'm Little Squirt.'

'Little Squirt and Biscuits,' Prickle-Head repeated. Pinch-Face snorted so enthusiastically that a bubble blew out of his nose.

'So, Biscuits,' said Prickle-Head. 'You like them, do you? Biscuits?'

'Yeah, I like them,' said Biscuits.

'Got any biscuits on you, then? How about sharing

them round?' said Prickle-Head.

'Sorry. I've eaten my last one,' said Biscuits. Then he added, *so* stupidly, 'And I wouldn't share them with you anyway.'

'You don't want to share your yummy Yoyos and wicked Wagon Wheels and heavenly Hob Nobs?' said Prickle-Head, tutting in a very ominous way. 'Well, we'll see about that. Go through the Fat Boy's pockets, Ricky. They're *bulging* with biscuits.'

'You keep your dirty hands off me,' said Biscuits, clenching his fists.

'Give them your biscuits, Biscuits. We'll get you some more later,' I hissed urgently. 'Don't try to fight them. You won't win.'

I was right. Biscuits hit out but he didn't manage to connect with anything. Prickle-Head kicked out and Biscuits doubled up, Pinch-Face pinioned his arms behind his back and pulled him upright.

I wanted to help him. I really did. But I didn't know *how*.

And I didn't want to get hurt.

Prickle-Head started poking in Biscuits' pockets. He found biscuits, sweets, chocolate, even a few crushed crisps.

'You greedy pig! You've got a whole corner shop stuffed down your trousers!' Prickle-Head yelled. He gave a last rootle and pulled out something

 91

squashed down right at the bottom of Biscuits' pocket. Something woolly.

'What on earth . . . ? Is this your little woolly cardi, Mummy's boy?' said Prickle-Head, shaking the strange pinky-grey object.

It sprouted floppy arms and legs. We were all looking at Dog Hog.

'It's a *cuddly toy*!' Prickle-Head shouted, hardly able to believe his luck.

Pinch-Face shrieked with glee.

Biscuits turned lobster red, as if he were being painfully boiled.

He tried to snatch Dog Hog back but Pinch-Face held him helpless.

I dithered on the edge, desperate. I craned round. Dad was *still* with the fishermen, examining their bait.

'*Dad!*' I yelled. 'Dad, come *here*!'

But it was windy on the pier. My voice only carried a few metres. Dad didn't hear me.

'Shut up, Little Squirt,' said Prickle-Head. 'Daddy's not coming and old Mumsie's gone missing. Oh boo-hoo, they want Mummy! Do you need a cuddle with your woolly whatsit, Fat-Bum?'

Prickle-Head dangled Dog Hog in front of Biscuits.

'What *is* it, anyway? It's all long and pink. Hey, is it a woolly willy?'

Pinch-Face squealed.

'Yes, tut, tut, a woolly willy. You don't want to play with a dirty old thing like that,' said Prickle-Head. He suddenly darted to the railings. He leaned over, holding Dog Hog between his finger and thumb.

'Don't!' Biscuits yelled.

'He's only pretending, Biscuits,' I said. '*Dad! Dad!* Look, I'll run for Dad, right?'

'Too late, Little Squirt,' said Prickle-Head, and he dropped Dog Hog over the side.

'Wheeeeee – splosh!' said Prickle-Head, and then he ran off laughing, his big boots thundering on the wooden planks. Pinch-Face ran after him, punching the air.

Biscuits and I rushed to the railings. He'd really dropped Dog Hog but not in the sea. There was a rotting landing stage directly below, and poor Dog Hog lay spread-eagled on it, splashed by the lapping sea.

Biscuits didn't hesitate. He seized the railings and swung his leg over.

'Biscuits! Don't be crazy! You can't! It's far too dangerous!' I yelled.

'I've got to get Dog Hog. I've had him since I was a baby. My nan knitted him.'

'Then she could knit you another one, Biscuits. Oh please, *don't*!'

'She can't knit another one. She's dead now. I *have* to get him, Tim,' said Biscuits, and he started climbing

 93

down determinedly.

'Biscuits! You might fall! *Please* don't. Wait for my dad,' I begged.

'I can't wait,' Biscuits gasped, and then his foot slipped on the wet railing and he was left hanging by his hands.

'*Biscuits!*'

Biscuits held on, got his feet back on the bar below, gave himself a second's breather, and then started feeling for the next bar – and the next – and the next. I hung over the pier, not daring to talk to him any more in case I distracted him. He went down and down – nearly slipped again, hung on – down and down – and then he jumped for it. He was there, on the landing stage!

It creaked ominously as he bounded onto it, as if it might break up altogether under his weight.

'Oh, be careful, Biscuits!' I whispered. Biscuits seized Dog Hog, held him briefly for one moment, and then stuffed him very firmly far down into his trouser pocket.

'There, I've got him!' said Biscuits. 'Now all I've got to do is get back.'

He looked up. He blinked.

'Ah. The thing is . . . *how* am I going to get back?' Biscuits said.

'I'll *have* to get Dad!' I shouted.

'Are you calling me, Tim?' It *was* Dad, suddenly right beside me. 'What is it? Where's Biscuits?'

'Down there!' I said, pointing.

'*What?*' Dad peered. 'Oh my goodness! Hang on, son. I'll come down.'

'No. I'll come up,' said Biscuits, and he spat on his palms determinedly. He seized the first bar and hauled.

'That's it!' said Dad. 'Now the next!'

Biscuits continued steadily, though his face was purple with effort.

'Steady now,' Dad cried. 'Biscuits? Are you all right? Here, I'm coming!'

'No! I'm – I'm – just – out – of – puff!' Biscuits gasped. 'But – I'm – OK.'

He looked down to see how far he'd got. He wavered.

'Don't look down!' Dad shouted.

Biscuits looked up, and started climbing again.

'That's the lad. Not too far now,' Dad said.

He looked over his shoulder. 'Thank heavens Mum's still with that fortune-teller. She'd go bananas if she saw Biscuits. What's he *playing* at? Don't you boys realize it's highly dangerous?'

'Yes, I realize it ever so, Dad,' I said. 'And so does Biscuits. But this was a serious emergency. You see these boys were being nasty to us and one of them—'

'OK, OK. Don't rabbit on about it now, Tim. Let's just concentrate on Biscuits getting back up here all in one piece,' said Dad, leaning right over and just about reaching Biscuits.

'Take my hand, Biscuits.'

Biscuits did as he was told. Dad very nearly toppled over with his weight, but just about managed to hang on. Biscuits climbed up, and Dad seized him under the armpits and hauled him back over the top of the railings.

Biscuits lay flat on the planks, gasping like the captured fish.

'Are you all right?' Dad asked. He sat down too, and mopped his brow.

'You – bet!' Biscuits puffed.

'Oh Biscuits, you were so *brave*!' I said.

'Yes – I was – wasn't I?' said Biscuits, sitting up and grinning.

'You were also very very reckless and silly,' said Dad. 'You must never ever do that again, do you promise?'

'Cross my heart and hope to die,' said Biscuits. 'Phew! I feel a bit peckish after all that high drama.'

Prickle-Head had dropped most of Biscuits' secret supply of food. Biscuits started gathering it up and consuming it rapidly.

I didn't feel hungry at all, even though I was

ultra-empty after being sick. I still felt bowled over by Biscuits' bravery. And cast down by my own cowardice.

I was a totally useless scaredy-cat little squirt.

I picked my way slowly back down the pier, plank by plank. Biscuits and Dad strode ahead, chatting man to man.

'Are you feeling all right, Tim?' said Mum, but she didn't sound too worried.

The fortune-teller had put her in an unusually good mood.

'She says I'm going to meet someone from the past – and romance is in the air,' said Mum, her eyes sparkling.

'I hope I don't breathe it in – I can't stick romance,' said Biscuits.

Dad laughed and patted him on the back. They decided they wanted to go to the amusement arcade. Dad bought us all candy floss. I didn't want mine so I gave it to Biscuits. He started playing this car chase with Dad. Mum began feeding coins into a fruit machine. She didn't listen properly when I started telling her about Prickle-Head and Pinch-Face.

'*What's* his name, darling?' Mum said vaguely – and then she laughed triumphantly. She'd won the jackpot.

'Oh, never mind,' I said huffily, and I wandered off by myself.

I stopped at one of those crane machines full of little rubber trolls with wild pink and purple hair. My girlfriend Kelly has a troll doll called Theresa.

I thought about Kelly. I hoped she wasn't still mad at me for asking Biscuits on holiday instead of her. I decided to try to win her another troll as a holiday present. A friend for Theresa. Yes, she'd really like that. She really liked me. Even if I wasn't very brave.

I put a whole pound coin in the machine. It gave me five goes. It should be easy-peasy to get one troll. Several. Maybe even five.

Ha! I wrestled with the handle that worked the crane but it wouldn't go where I wanted. It missed altogether the first two goes. It caught a troll's hair the third go and I gasped – but the troll slipped away. I missed the fourth time. My hand started to shake for the fifth and final go.

Someone was standing behind me, watching. I *hate* that. The crane opened up its claws. It brushed against a couple of trolls. It knocked one so that its little rubber arm waved cheekily. But then the claws closed on nothing. The crane went up again – empty.

'You're pretty useless!' someone said. 'Here, you'd better let me have a go.'

I turned round to look at this rude stranger.

It wasn't a stranger at all.

It was Kelly!!!

Tim's diary

Kelly says she is still my girlfriend. She is a lot of fun. But a bit tiring.

I think Biscuits is glad Kelly is not his girlfriend.

I am a bit worried because if you have a girlfriend I think you are supposed to protect her from Deadly Enemies. I am useless at this. Kelly says, who cares? She will protect me from Deadly Enemies.

The Enemy is getting deadlier every day.

Yoo hoo!

Maybe we both need to be protected.

Biscuits' diary

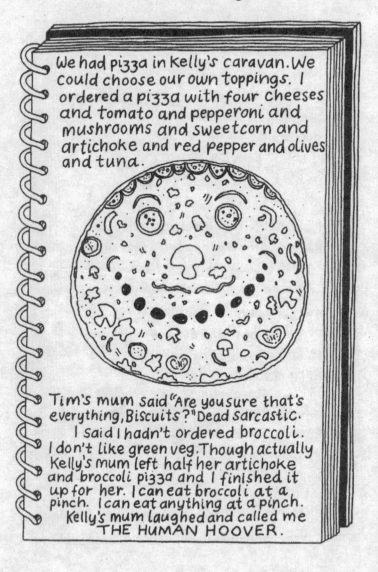

We had pizza in Kelly's caravan. We could choose our own toppings. I ordered a pizza with four cheeses and tomato and pepperoni and mushrooms and sweetcorn and artichoke and red pepper and olives and tuna.

Tim's mum said "Are you sure that's everything, Biscuits?" Dead sarcastic.

I said I hadn't ordered broccoli. I don't like green veg. Though actually Kelly's mum left half her artichoke and broccoli pizza and I finished it up for her. I can eat broccoli at a pinch. I can eat anything at a pinch.

Kelly's mum laughed and called me THE HUMAN HOOVER.

☆ CHAPTER FOUR ☆

I couldn't believe it was Kelly. But there are no other girls like her. She has hair sticking straight up in the air in a top knot. When she's excited it waggles about. She's got little dark glinty eyes and a great big grin. She wears bright clingy clothes and posh trainers and she talks all the time. Well, I suppose there *are* quite a lot of girls like Kelly, but she's the bounciest.

'Kelly!' I said.

'Hi, Tim,' she said. She grinned, the corners of her mouth almost tickling her ears. She had new earrings, white and sparkly. She twiddled them proudly.

'Do you like my diamonds? My mum's boyfriend Dave bought me them as a holiday present,' she said.

'Wow! Real diamonds!' I said.

'Well. Not *real* real. But they're very good synthetic stones,' Kelly said, tossing her head about so that they caught the light. 'Right. Budge over, Tim. I'll show you how to work these cranes.'

Kelly's mum's boyfriend Dave had given her a whole purseful of change. She inserted a coin and started twiddling.

She was *ace*.

In a matter of minutes Theresa Troll had a whole tribe of relations: Tracy Troll and Truman Troll and Tabitha Troll and Tyrone Troll and Tilly Troll and Trocadero Troll. Biscuits and Dad and Mum heard Kelly's triumphant crowing as she kept capturing yet another troll. They came over to watch.

Then Kelly's mum and Kelly's mum's boyfriend Dave and Kelly's little brother Dean and her baby brother Keanu came and watched too. It got very crowded. I'd have died if everyone was watching me. It didn't put Kelly off a bit.

Then all the grown-ups started talking and Kelly's mum's new boyfriend Dave got introduced. He had the most amazing tattoos all the way up his arms. Snakes and flowers and hearts and a lady in a bikini. He could make her waggle when he moved his muscle. He showed Biscuits and me and we thought it cooler than cool. We kept wanting him to do it, but Mum gave me a sharp nudge and told me not to keep pestering. She didn't say much else. Kelly's mum said lots and lots. Dad did too.

'I just can't get over the coincidence of you being here on holiday too!' he said. 'I mean, Llanpistyll and Abercoch are such out of the way places.'

'It was our Kelly. She looked them up on the map, she did, and said she just *knew* Llanpistyll would be great. And so we made sure there was a caravan site – and here we are.'

'Oh, you're staying at the caravan site,' said Mum.

'Don't tell me you are too!' said Kelly's mum, laughing and flipping her pony-tail.

Kelly's mum is ever so like Kelly. Only more glittery.

'Oh no! No, we're staying at the Gwesty Bryn Nodfa. It's a very nice quiet family hotel,' said Mum.

'Poor you,' said Kelly. 'It's ever such fun down the caravan site. We've got our *own* amusement arcade and there's swings and all sorts.'

'Yes, it's great for the kiddies,' said Kelly's mum's boyfriend Dave. 'They can amuse themselves. And we can amuse *our*selves.'

'You must come over. Come now!' Kelly said.

'Can we, Mum?' I said.

'Oh no, dear. No, we're going to look at another castle,' Mum said quickly.

'Then come for tea,' said Kelly.

'Ooh, let's,' said Biscuits.

'No, I'm sorry, we have our evening meal at our hotel,' said Mum.

'*Supper*, then,' said Kelly.

'Please!' I said.

'Double please with knobs on,' said Biscuits.

Mum opened her mouth. It was already in a firm No shape. But guess what!

'*Yes*,' said Dad. 'Yes, we'd love to.'

'But we won't have finished our meal till seven at the earliest,' said Mum. 'And then the boys should really be in bed by half-past seven.'

'You go to bed at half-past *seven*?' said Kelly. 'I don't go to bed till twelve sometimes, isn't that right, Mum?'

'We go to bed *later* than that,' said Dean.

'And this little monkey stays up *all* night sometimes,' said Kelly's mum, picking up Keanu and giving him a little toss in the air.

Keanu squealed and drool came out of his mouth and dripped down onto Kelly's mum.

'You little whatsit!' she said. 'Are you spitting at your mum, eh? I'll give you what for.' She tossed him up in the air again and he squealed and slurped again.

Biscuits and I watched in appalled fascination.

'I don't really reckon babies,' said Biscuits.

'Me too,' I said.

'Me *three*,' said Kelly. 'You try living with one all the time. So – you're coming round to the site, right?'

It was all agreed.

Mum was narked and had words with Dad back at

the hotel. Lots and lots of words. We could easily hear them in the next room.

I felt fussed about Biscuits.

'It's OK, Super-Tim,' he said kindly. 'You should hear my mum going on at my dad sometimes.'

I felt a lot better. Though I was a bit worried about going to the caravan site myself.

'Why don't you want to go now? Kelly's your girlfriend, isn't she?' said Biscuits. He made kissy-kissy noises.

'Shut up. I don't *kiss* her.'

'Oh darling Kelly, You've got such a flat belly, You're never ever smelly, Let's sit in the dark and watch telly,' said Biscuits, clasping Dog Hog. He made Dog Hog wiggle around and say in a squeaky voice: 'Oh Tim, Tim, You're not so dim, Come and cuddle in.'

'You nut! Shut up, shut up,' I said, seizing Dog Hog and bashing Biscuits on the head with him.

'Ouch! Kelly's attacking me,' Biscuits giggled.

'Well, give it a rest, you pest. Oh no! You've got me doing daft rhymes now. No, about the caravan site. I was thinking . . . what if Prickle-Head and Pinch-Face hang out round there?'

'Ah,' said Biscuits. He smoothed Dog Hog and laid him down gently on his pillow. 'I don't think I'll take him with me then.'

'He can keep Walter company,' I said. 'Biscuits, you

were so brave rescuing Dog Hog. I wish I was brave like you.'

'Well, if Prickle-Head threw Walter Bear over the railings you'd go and get him, wouldn't you?' said Biscuits.

'Mmm,' I said doubtfully. 'I *hope* I would. I don't know though. I wish I wasn't such a coward.'

'You're not really,' said Biscuits – but he sounded doubtful too.

'Yes, I am. I'm afraid of everything.'

'Look, *I'm* afraid of Prickle-Head,' said Biscuits. 'And Pinch-Face too. He didn't half dig his nails in when he had hold of me.'

'I'm afraid of heaps of other people too. I even get scared of my dad sometimes.'

'Your dad? That's daft, your dad's smashing. It's your mum who's a bit . . .'

'A bit what?'

'Oh, never mind.'

'OK, I'm not scared of my mum. But I'm scared of all these *things* too.'

'*What* things?' said Biscuits. He pulled a face and made his fingers into scrabbly claws. 'Ghosties and ghoulies?'

'Silly things. Like looking down from the top of the castle. And – and the cracks in the pier. And all sorts of other stuff.' I sighed miserably. 'I'm a complete wimp.'

 106

'You're a tearful wimp – and I'm a cheerful chimp!' said Biscuits, suddenly straddling his legs and letting his arms hang loose. He made loud chimpanzee noises. 'Me want bananas!'

It was impossible to stay depressed around Biscuits.

'Me want bananas too!' I said, and did my own chimp impersonation.

Then we grew into Giant Gorillas and did mating calls and Mum stopped telling Dad off next door to come and tell us off instead.

'You're obviously getting very silly and over-tired already,' she said. 'It's *not* a good idea for us all to traipse over to this caravan site after tea. But as your father has committed us then I suppose we've no option. But we're not going to stay long. We'll just say hello and stop ten minutes to be polite. We certainly won't want any supper.'

'Some of us might!' said Biscuits.

Mum pretended not to hear. She wasn't talking to Dad at all when we drove over to the caravan site. I was a bit quiet myself, still worried that we might meet up with Prickle-Head any moment. I peered round anxiously as we walked down the rows of caravans – and then someone leapt on my back!

'Hey, Tim, it's me!' Kelly said. 'What are you screaming about?'

 107

'You made me jump,' I gasped. 'Don't creep up on me like that again, Kelly.'

'Oh, go on, it's fun,' said Kelly. 'Hi, everyone. Our caravan's at the back, over by the oak trees. This way!'

She directed us like a traffic policeman. A big boy with short hair suddenly ran down the steps of his caravan and I stopped still, my heart thudding – but it wasn't Prickle-Head after all, just some mild mini look-alike.

'Do you know him?' said Kelly. 'He was sucking up to me down the swings last night. But I told him I wasn't interested.'

'Really?' I said, cheering up a little. 'No, I don't know him. But there's this other boy from somewhere round here—'

'A friend of yours, is he?'

'He's a Deadly Enemy, him and his mate. They keep getting us, Biscuits and me.'

'What's he done to you then?'

'Well. First of all he kicked my . . .'

'He *kicked* you?'

'No, he didn't kick me. He kicked my sandcastle.' I felt silly saying it. I sounded like a really little kid. 'It wasn't an ordinary sandcastle. It was a proper motte and bailey castle and I'd spent hours building it. And then they attacked us on the pier. It was really scary, Kelly, I thought they were going to throw us right over

108

into the water. They were teasing Biscuits and they dropped Dog Hog over the railings.'

'But I bet you rescued him like you rescued my Theresa Troll, right?' said Kelly.

'Wrong,' I said. 'I was useless. Biscuits rescued him himself. He was brilliantly brave, Kelly. But even Biscuits is scared of Prickle-Head.'

'Prickle-Head!' said Kelly, snorting. 'Look, don't you worry, Tim. If this Prickle-Head bobs up and starts giving you bother *I'll* sort him out for you, OK?'

'OK,' I said, and we shook hands on it.

We carried on holding hands as we walked over to Kelly's caravan. It felt . . . odd. I've held hands before. Mum's. This was *very* different. It felt OK. Yet I was scared of Biscuits seeing and laughing. And I was scared my palm might get all hot and sweaty. And I was scared to move my fingers about in case Kelly thought I was trying to tickle her but my hand was so rigid it felt like a baseball mitt. *Scared* again.

'That's our caravan,' Kelly yelled, dropping my hand and dancing forward without a second thought.

I wish wish wish I was a person without a second thought. I have *third* thoughts. But for a while *all* my thoughts were absorbed in admiring Kelly's caravan.

It was all so neat and tidy and dinky and perfect, like the best Wendy House in the world. I especially liked the way the table folded up and the bed folded down.

'That's Dean's bed. When he's being a right pain I shove the bed back into the wall with him inside,' said Kelly.

Even Mum seemed impressed with the proper flushing toilet and the television and the frilly curtains up at the window.

'It's like a little palace,' she said politely.

'And here's my princess,' said Kelly's mum's boyfriend Dave, and he put his arm round Kelly's mum and squeezed her tight.

'Get off of me,' she said, but you could tell she was pleased.

Kelly pulled a *yuck* face at Biscuits and me.

'Do you want a Coke, you two? We've got lots in the fridge.'

'You've even got a fridge!' said Mum.

We all had drinks. Dad and Kelly's mum's boyfriend Dave had a can of beer. Mum said, '*No*, thank you' when she got offered a beer too.

'I know what you'd like,' said Kelly's mum.

Mum's eyebrows went up as if she didn't think that very likely.

'I'm not really a drinker,' she murmured, as Kelly's mum produced a bottle of Baileys.

'You try a drop of this,' said Kelly's mum. 'Got a

 110

sweet tooth, have you? It tastes just like chocolate.'

'Like chocolate!' said Biscuits. 'Can I have some too?'

Kelly's mum gave him one weeny sip. Mum looked horrified – but when she took an even weenier sip of her own glassful she looked surprised. She didn't say anything, but she drank it all up. *And* had another glass after that.

It seemed to put her in a good mood because she didn't say no when we all ordered take-away pizzas on Kelly's mum's boyfriend Dave's mobile phone.

'I'd never have thought I'd be ordering a pizza in Llanpistyll,' said Dad.

'Well, don't get too excited. We ordered them last night and the first lot went astray,' said Kelly's mum. 'Some of them little toerags waylaid the guy on the pizza-bike. Honestly! Kids nowadays!'

All the grown-ups started in on one of those yawny-yawny kids-of-today conversations while Dean showed us all his toys. I started fooling around with his Lego bricks and made him a little castle.

'Oh wow! That's great, Tim,' said Kelly. 'Make one for me, eh?'

The four of us played with the Lego. Baby Keanu kept trying to smash everything in sight. Then he mistook a red Lego brick for a baby rusk and rammed it in his mouth. He did his best to swallow. He started to turn as red as the brick.

 111

'Keanu's choking,' said Kelly calmly, and she tipped him upside down and thumped him on the back.

The brick came shooting out like a bullet. Keanu crowed happily, none the worse.

'That's some party trick, Kelly,' I said. 'Does he often swallow things?'

'All the time,' said Kelly. 'Hey, I wonder what you were like as a baby, Biscuits! I bet you stuffed *everything* in your little gob. Bricks, rubber dollies, your own little booties . . .'

'His dummy, yum yum, chew chew, swallow! His baby bottle, yum yum, crunch crunch, swallow! Hey, his *pottie*, yum yum *OUCH*!'

Biscuits was doing his best to turn *me* upside down, but mercifully the pizzas arrived just at that moment. We *all* went yum yum, munch munch. We ate outdoors because the caravan was quite a squash with eight and a half people shut inside. Lots of other people were sitting outside their caravans chatting and eating and drinking. Kelly and her family had only arrived yesterday but already everyone knew them. Some kids came over and asked if Kelly was coming over to the swings with them.

'Maybe later. I've got my friends here, see,' said Kelly. 'Isn't that right, Tim?'

'Sure, Kelly,' I said, pleased to be singled out as Kelly's special friend.

Biscuits didn't mind. He was busy with his second pizza. But then Dad went and spoilt it all.

'Why don't you all play together, eh? How about a game of French cricket? I'll show you how to play if you like.'

'Oh no,' I mumbled. 'Please don't let's play, Dad.'

'I shall get hiccups if I have to play,' said Biscuits, his mouth full.

'I don't want to play with those kids anyway, they're boring,' said Kelly.

Dad didn't listen to any of us. He started careering round looking for a bat and ball. He couldn't find a bat at all and the only ball was a red and yellow stripy one belonging to Keanu. He'd just started the mammoth task of hugging it to his chest and licking it all over and he didn't appreciate Dad taking it. Not one bit.

'There must be an old cricket bat somewhere,' said Dad.

'Sorry, mate. Not my cup of tea, cricket,' said Kelly's mum's boyfriend Dave.

'What about using my umbrella?' said Kelly's mum, hitching the howling Keanu onto her hip. 'Oh do put a sock in it, young man! Kelly, find my brolly.'

Kelly nipped inside the caravan and came out with a very fancy spotty umbrella. She aimed it at a stone with a nifty little swing.

'Watch it, Kelly! Maybe that umbrella's a bit fragile.'

'Let's play golf instead of cricket,' said Kelly,

giving another stone a whack. Then she squealed, her pony-tail waving like a flag as she jumped up and down.

'*I* know! Let's go and play Crazy Golf. Let's, let's, let's!'

'How can you play Crazy Golf now, dear? It's nearly dark,' said Mum, looking at her watch. 'Oh my goodness, we'd better be getting back to the hotel.'

'No, one of the kids on the site told me, you can play it by floodlight. Oh *please*!'

'No, I don't really think—' Mum started.

'Just one quick round. And it's on us,' said Dad.

There'd been a lot of adult argy-bargy about who was paying for the pizzas. Kelly's mum's boyfriend Dave had won. Mum was mega-fussed about it, so she couldn't really back out of the Crazy Golf idea, seeing as it was now our treat.

There was just one problem. One huge enormous disastrous drawback.

'I've never played Crazy Golf!' I said.

'Neither have I – but it's great,' said Kelly.

'Have you played Crazy Golf, Biscuits?' I asked.

'Nope. Like the sound of Crazy. Not too nuts about the Golf bit though,' said Biscuits, easing the waistband on his straining tracksuit trousers.

'We all need a bit of exercise,' said Dad, patting his

own tummy. He seized Kelly's mum's umbrella and did a fancy golf swing of his own.

'Oooh, I can see we've got an expert here,' said Kelly's mum, fluttering her eyelashes at him.

Dad gave a silly laugh and then patted baby Keanu on the head. Keanu howled harder.

I felt like howling myself when we got to the Crazy Golf. It was brilliantly lit up by floodlight, with heaps of people playing. The course was huge, with little waterfalls trickling here and there, and all sorts of twisty bits and hidey holes and hill-ocks. There was a wide wall all the way round the course so that people could peer over and gawp at the golfers.

Dad was a bit taken aback when he saw how much it was, but he said, swallowing hard, that he'd like tickets for seven players, him and Mum, Kelly's mum and Kelly's mum's boyfriend Dave, Kelly herself and Biscuits and me.

'*And me!*' Dean said, outraged. 'Me play too! I can play, can't I, Mum, *can't I*?'

'Of course you can play. Sorry, pal, I just didn't realize you were big enough,' said Dad.

'I'm *ever* so big,' said Dean, standing on tip-toe.

I was huddling up in horror.

'Dad, just get seven tickets. I won't play,' I said.

'What? Of course you're playing, Tim,' said Dad.

 115

'But I don't want to,' I hissed. 'I can't play Crazy Golf. I'll be useless.'

'Don't be silly, Tim. It's *fun*,' said Dad. Everyone else thought it was fun. We were all given golf clubs, big ones for the grown-ups, middley ones for Biscuits and Kelly and me, and a little one for Dean. He waved it above his head excitedly. It caught me on the chin. It hurt a *lot* but Dad gave me a warning glance and I couldn't say anything much.

Kelly had first go and she hit the ball so hard it whizzed right across the first green, hit the wall at the end, and went socking straight back to where she'd started. I went bright red on her behalf but she just laughed.

'That was just a practice shot!' she said, and had another go.

This time her aim was perfect. She hit the ball so that it whizzed up the little slope but slowed down in time so that it stopped almost on the edge of the hole.

'Wow! I'm good at this!' Kelly yelled immodestly.

Her mum was even better. She passed Keanu over to my mum, hardly bothered to take aim, gave the ball a sharp little tap – and got a hole in one!

'Well done, well done!' said Dad, and patted her on the back.

Dave gave her a great-big-kiss-on-the-lips – a very different sort of kiss from the kind Dad gives Mum.

 116

Mum didn't look in a kissy mood at all. She thrust Keanu at Dad and took aim. She didn't get a hole in one. Or two or three or four. Dad kept telling her to hold her club at a different angle and Mum's lips got tighter and her knuckles whiter as she gripped the club and whacked. Her score was six.

Dean scored six too. He did much better than I'd expect of a little kid his age.

Then Kelly's mum's boyfriend Dave had a go and he scored *another* hole in one. There was another great-big-kiss-on-the-lips. They even made *noises*. Biscuits imitated them delightedly. Mum nudged him and frowned. I'd have died of embarrassment if I was Kelly but she just laughed and said if they went on like that she'd have to tip them in the waterfall to cool them off.

Then it was Dad's turn. He still had Keanu. He tried to pass him over to Biscuits and me, but we backed away. Kelly rescued us and took him herself. Dad took a long time, bending his knees and peering at the hole and swinging his club around.

'Come on, mate, get on with it,' Kelly's mum's boyfriend Dave said, wiping Kelly's mum's lipstick off his chin.

Dad looked a little irritated and hit the ball. He didn't get a hole in one. Or two. He scored three.

'Here, I thought you were meant to be an ace golfer!' said Kelly's mum's boyfriend Dave, looking amused.

'Yes, but no one can play properly on these little Mickey Mouse greens,' Dad said quickly. 'Come on, boys, get a move on. We're holding up the next players.'

I turned round and saw to my horror there was a little queue of people waiting to start their game. They'd all be watching me.

'I don't want to play!' I mumbled.

'You might be good at golf,' said Biscuits cheerily. 'Shall I go next then?'

Biscuits was brilliant! He very nearly got a hole in one himself, but it just bounced over it. He sank the ball with just one more quick putt.

'Wowie! *I'm* good at golf!' said Biscuits, doing a little joggy up and down dance, making everyone laugh.

I was glad for him – and yet I wished he'd made a real muck-up of it. Then I wouldn't be the worst.

'Come on, Tim,' Dad yelled at me. 'Everyone's waiting.'

'Look, it's OK, I won't play,' I said. 'I don't mind a bit. I don't want to make all these people wait.'

'Don't be so silly, Tim,' said Dad, and he came striding over to me. He lowered his head. 'Don't show me up in front of all the others,' he hissed. 'Just get on with it.'

I tried. My hands were slippy as I seized the club. I took a wild swing. And missed completely.

 118

'Hey, hey, careful!' said Dad. 'No, you've got to keep your eye on the ball. Have another go.'

I tried. I did hit the ball this time. About a centimetre.

'Hit it a bit *harder*, Tim,' said Dad, sighing. 'And hold the club with your hands together. No wonder you're so useless.'

I tried again. I could hear giggling behind me. Kelly and Biscuits were talking together, looking at me.

It was cold in the moonlight, with a sharp breeze off the sea, but I was burning hot. I took another swing and the ball went careering off in totally the wrong direction.

There was a great scornful whoop. Not from behind. Not from in front. From above. I looked up. *It was Prickle-Head and Pinch-Face!*

'Oh no. Oh Dad, please. I can't play any more. Don't make me,' I begged.

'Just do your best,' Dad said.

'But those boys, they're watching me.'

'Take no notice.'

I took another swing. How can you take no notice when your worst enemies in the world are cracking up laughing because you're so hopeless?

Mum started walking towards me, looking cross. Oh no. It was getting worse.

'You boys up there! You mind your own business!' she shouted.

They hooted even harder. I took one last desperate shot and missed again.

'What a load of rubbish!' yelled Prickle-Head, and then he took his Coke can and threw it at me. 'Rubbish, rubbish, rubbish! Throw your rubbish at the rubbish!'

'*Right!*' said Dad. Kelly's mum's boyfriend Dave was coming over too.

Prickle-Head and Pinch-Face decided to make a run for it.

'But we're still going to *get* you,' Prickle-Head yelled. 'You just w-a-i-t!'

Tim's diary

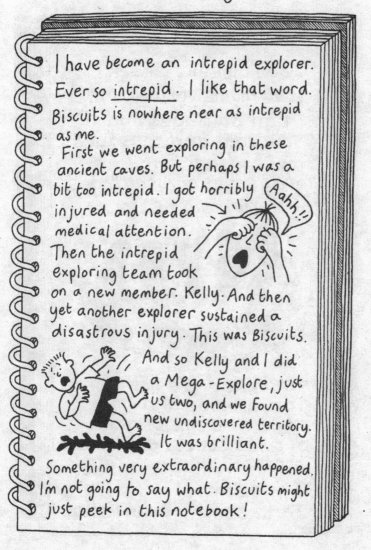

I have become an intrepid explorer. Ever so intrepid. I like that word. Biscuits is nowhere near as intrepid as me.

First we went exploring in these ancient caves. But perhaps I was a bit too intrepid. I got horribly injured and needed medical attention.

Aahh!!

Then the intrepid exploring team took on a new member. Kelly. And then yet another explorer sustained a disastrous injury. This was Biscuits.

And so Kelly and I did a Mega-Explore, just us two, and we found new undiscovered territory. It was brilliant.

Something very extraordinary happened. I'm not going to say what. Biscuits might just peek in this notebook!

Biscuits' diary

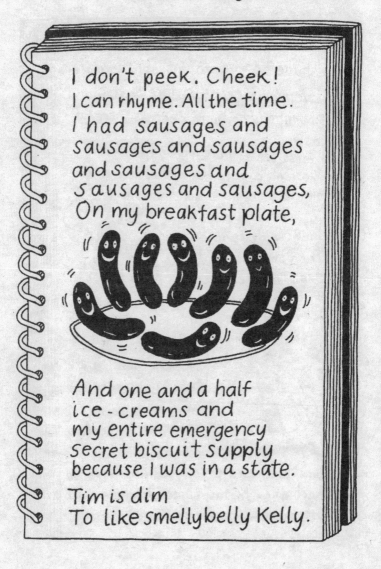

I don't peek. Cheek!
I can rhyme. All the time.
I had sausages and
sausages and sausages
and sausages and
sausages and sausages,
On my breakfast plate,

And one and a half
ice-creams and
my entire emergency
secret biscuit supply
because I was in a state.

Tim is dim
To like smellybelly Kelly.

✰ CHAPTER FIVE ✰

I went up and up and up the tower steps, gasping for breath. There was someone behind me. I could hear them getting nearer and nearer.

I kept craning back fearfully but it was so dark and I couldn't see anything. But there was a faint glimmer ahead. I was nearly at the top.

I made one last desperate effort and stepped out onto the castle battlements, my hands ready to clasp the wall . . . *but it wasn't there!*

I was standing on a tiny parapet, the wind whistling around me. If I took just one step forward I'd be treading thin air!

'*Where's the wall?*'

There was a horrible laugh from behind me. I turned my head stiffly, not daring to move any more in case I toppled over.

Prickle-Head was grinning at me from the doorway. He stamped his huge boots.

'These are great for kicking. A few kicks at that wall and it crumbled. You're the one that's going to crumble now, Mummy's Boy. You like cissy pretend games, don't you? Well, you can play at being a weathercock now. Have fun!'

He dodged back and slammed the door shut. I heard the thud and rattle as he bolted it from the inside.

'Please! Come back! You can't do this!' I screamed.

'I *said* I was going to get you,' Prickle-Head shouted from behind the door.

I heard the clump of his boots down and down and down the steps.

I was left, unable to move, my head spinning, eyes streaming, mouth screaming. It was so windy I could barely keep my balance. I had to keep still, it was my only chance, but I was being buffeted from side to side, and I felt so sick and dizzy I couldn't keep my legs stiff. I staggered forward, arms flailing wildly – and then I fell.

Down, down, down . . .

and landed with a bump.

'Tim?'

'Oooh!'

'What're you doing on the floor?'

'I fell out of bed. I think I was having a nightmare.'

'Oh. Right. Night then,' said Biscuits.

Walter Bear had fallen with me. I clutched him tight against my chest.

'Tim?' said Biscuits.

'What?'

'Why aren't you getting back into bed?'

'Because – because I don't want to go back to sleep. In case the nightmare comes back.'

'Was it a really awful maniac-killer-with-a-machine-gun nightmare?' said Biscuits.

'Worse!'

'Wow. Well. Do you want to get in my bed for a bit?'

'Yes please,' I said.

It wasn't very comfortable in Biscuits' bed. Biscuits himself took up a great deal of room, and his sheets were all prickly with crumbs. But it was much much cosier squashed up with him than my own cold bed where the Prickle-Head dream was still lurking, ready to flash on the screen in my head the minute I closed my eyes.

Walter Bear had also crept in with me. He cuddled up with Dog Hog.

'Is Tim feeling better now?' said Dog Hog.

'Much better, thank you,' said Walter.

'He doesn't *sound* much better. Tell him not to worry. It was only a nightmare. It can't come true,' said Dog Hog.

 125

'It can,' said Walter. 'He says it's about Prickle-Head.'

'Ah,' said Dog Hog. '*Him*.'

'Yes,' said Walter Bear. 'He's going to get Tim.'

'And Biscuits,' said Dog Hog.

'He's going to get me *more*,' I said in my ordinary voice, forgetting to be Walter Bear. 'He chased me up this castle and then left me right at the top and there was nothing to hold on to and it was so awful—'

'But he couldn't really do that,' said Biscuits.

'Well, all right. But he could . . .' I paused, thinking of 1001 possibilities.

'He can't do anything really,' said Biscuits firmly. 'Not with your mum and dad around. Especially not your mum.' He chuckled.

I started laughing too, but a little uneasily.

'I suppose he can't actually *kill* me,' I said. 'But – but he can still call me horrible names.'

'We can call him horrible names back,' said Biscuits. 'I know! Let's have a Horrible Names for Prickle-Head contest!'

This was enormous fun. We started off mildly enough:

Pea-brain Prickle-Head. Pig-manure Prickle-Head. Pukey Prickle-Head.

Then the names got longer and fancier and much much ruder.

 126

We were soon shaking with laughter, so that we were both in danger of tumbling right out of bed.

Then I suddenly heard a bedroom door slam. Footsteps, rapidly approaching!

'Help!' I hissed, and I shot out of Biscuits' bed and into my own.

'What on *earth* are you two boys playing at!' Mum whispered fiercely, bursting into our room. 'It's four o'clock in the morning and you're waking the whole hotel!'

I kept my eyes shut and tried to breathe evenly, though my heart was thudding. Biscuits gave a very realistic little snore.

'You can't fool me,' said Mum – but she sounded uncertain.

She waited . . . and then we heard her tip-toeing out.

I felt the most desperate giggle shaking my whole body. I had to go down under the sheets to muffle it. Biscuits was snorting too. A little too loudly.

'Sh! She'll come back! We'd better go to sleep now,' I said.

'But I'm wide awake,' said Biscuits. 'And I'm *starving*. I'm going to ask for double sausages at breakfast. *Triple*.'

He did too. Mrs Jones laughed delightedly and called him Little Lord Greedyguts.

 127

'Anything to oblige and fill the Royal Tum,' she said, bustling off to the kitchen.

Biscuits and I laughed too, but Mum frowned. She wasn't in a good mood anyway because of her disturbed night.

'Really, Biscuits! It's very rude of you to keep asking Mrs Jones for more food. She gives you very generous portions as it is. You mustn't do it.'

'But she *likes* it when I ask for more. She thinks it's funny,' Biscuits protested.

'Well, I don't think it's funny at all,' said Mum. 'And you can't possibly want any more sausages. You'll be sick.'

'I'm never sick,' said Biscuits. 'Even on the day I had a Christmas dinner with my mum and dad and then we went to my auntie's and we had another whole Christmas dinner with her and then we went to my gran's in the evening and we had a big buffet and I ate *all* the sausages on sticks, every single one. I wasn't sick then. And I wasn't even sick on my birthday when—'

'*I'm* getting sick of this subject,' said Mum.

Mrs Jones was coming back with a plate of sizzling sausages, so Mum was forced to smile and be extra grateful.

Biscuits tucked into the sausages. He ate them all. The whole plateful. And then he smacked his lips happily.

'When you die they'll pickle your stomach and doctors will come and look at it and *marvel*,' I said.

Biscuits still looked hopefully at the ice-cream stall as we went on the beach, but after one glance at Mum he could see there was no point asking.

Dad made a great to-do of getting the deckchairs positioned and the windbreak up.

'You're probably wasting your time. It looks as if it's going to start raining,' said Mum, eyeing the grey sky.

'Nonsense!' said Dad. 'The sun's just about to break through, you'll see.'

Mum sniffed, pulled on another cardigan, and got her book out of her beach-bag. Dad reached for his paper, taking great deep breaths to show he was appreciating the balmy air, though there were goose pimples from the end of his shorts to his ankles.

'You two boys had better run about a bit to get warm,' Mum said.

'I'm warm enough,' said Biscuits, getting out his comic.

I read my own comic for a bit, and then I got my drawing book and doodled around doing a picture strip of me and Biscuits being Super-Tim and Biscuits-Boy. Super-Tim swooped up to the castle battlements and rescued damsels in distress who were swooningly grateful. He rounded up evil enemies, conquering them with a swift chop to the chops. 'Kerpow!' said

 129

Super-Tim and 'Wow!' said Biscuits-Boy, marvelling at his best friend's bravery and brawn.

'What are you drawing?' said Biscuits, peering over my shoulder.

'Just silly rubbish,' I said, crumpling the page quickly. 'Come on, Biscuits, let's do something. Let's go looking for shells and seaweed and stuff and then identify it from my seaside nature book.'

'That sounds like super fun – *not!*' said Biscuits. 'Just like school.'

'No, we might find something mega-rare. Some extraordinary lugworm all coiled up in the sand and we'll start digging him up and find he's vast, one of the great loathly worms they had in the Middle Ages. Or – or we'll pick up this ordinary old stone and we'll see all the markings on it and it'll be a Stone Age flint used by a caveman to make an axe to attack all the woolly mammoths and sabre-tooth tigers. Aah! I've got a better idea! Let's find a cave and explore it and see if we can find any cave paintings.'

'No, let's find a cave that long-ago pirates used and they hid their ill-gotten gains in it, gold coins and jewels and stuff, and we'll find it in a rotting old trunk and live like lottery winners for ever,' said Biscuits.

'OK, OK, well, the cave could have both,' I said. 'Let's find it, eh? Explorers' gear required, Biscuits-Boy.'

'Aye, aye, Super-Tim.'

We got the spades and ran up the beach to where the sand dunes started teetering upwards in an uneven cliff. Little sandmartins flew in and out of an entire birdy housing estate right up at the top. There were a few shallow cubby-holes at the bottom of the cliff, but none that could be seriously described as caves.

'We'll have to tunnel to discover the secret entrance,' I said, attacking the soft sand vigorously with my spade.

'Oh oh! Hard labour time again. Can't you summon up your superhuman powers and blast your way through to save them?' said Biscuits, sitting on the handle of his spade. 'Then I can sit here and have a bit of a rest.'

'You can't have a rest now. You haven't done any work. Come on, let's get digging.'

But as we both set to, Mum started shouting at us. Something about Silly and Dangerous and Stop-it-at-once.

'What's she on about now?' Biscuits muttered. 'Maybe you're not supposed to dig on a full stomach?'

'That's swimming,' I said. 'No, maybe she's worried that we might get sand in our eyes. Actually, I already have, it's all gritty.'

I blinked. Mum loomed large through a hazy blur.

'You *silly* boys! You mustn't *ever* tunnel in sandcliffs like that. It's terribly dangerous. The sand can easily

 131

shift and fall on top of you and trap you. Never ever do that. Tim? Why are you screwing up your face like that? Oh darling, have you got sand in your eye?'

She tried making me blow my nose but it didn't work.

'It's OK,' I said, hating the fuss Mum was making in front of Biscuits. 'It's fine now,' I pretended, giving my eye a quick rub with my fist.

This was a serious mistake. My eye suddenly felt as if it was being scrubbed with emery-paper.

'Oh dear goodness. Hold still, Tim. Oh, your poor eye,' Mum said, as I hopped about in agony, my eye squeezed shut, tears seeping down my cheeks.

'Don't carry on like that, Tim, it's just a speck of sand,' said Dad, coming over. Then he had a proper look. 'Oh dear. It looks like you've got half the beach in there, old son. We need some water to wash it out.'

'I'll get a bucket and get some sea-water,' said Biscuits.

'No, dear – it's salty, that's no use. Come with me, Tim,' said Mum. 'I'll have to take you back to the hotel and we'll use a proper eye bath.'

So Mum whisked me off while Biscuits and Dad stayed on the beach. I tried to stop crying, terrified that Prickle-Head and Pinch-Face might bob up out of nowhere and call me a cissy crybaby, but my eye hurt so much I couldn't help it.

'You poor darling,' Mum said distractedly, as we stumbled across the cabbage field and down the windy footpaths. 'I'll get them to phone for a doctor when we get to the hotel. Or maybe it would be better to dial 999 for an ambulance. You can't be too careful with eyes. I think you should go to the hospital.'

I started crying harder. By the time we got to the hotel we were both convinced I was going to end up blind in both eyes. Mum was crying too.

'What's the matter? Has the little lad had an accident?' said Mrs Jones. 'Oh dear, sand in his eye, is it? Don't you fret, we'll sort it out in no time.'

She picked me up in her big strong arms as if I were no bigger than baby Keanu. She swept me into her kitchen, sat me down on her draining board, and ran some cold water into a cup. She held it against my hurting eye, tipped my head back, and told me to open the sore eye as wide as possible. It stopped hurting quite so badly. She did it again. It got much better. She had a good peer into my eye, gently holding it wide open.

'Aha! There's one little gritty bit left. We'll get it out in half a tick, you'll see.' She took the corner of her linen tea-towel and gave a quick flick.

'That's it!' she said triumphantly. 'Now, one more rinse for luck and you'll be as right as rain, young man.'

'It's stopped hurting! Well, it's still a bit sore, but it's much much better,' I said, blinking happily.

She still felt I should see a doctor to make sure my eye was really all right, but it would mean going all the way to Abercoch to the nearest health centre.

'We don't want to do that, Mum, it would take all morning,' I said.

'We could have a quick look round the shops while we were there. We didn't really get a proper chance last time with your dad and your pal Biscuits.'

'I want to go back on the beach, Mum! Please!'

Mum sighed. 'All right then, dear. But I can't quite see the charm of Llanpistyll beach myself. It's not even sunny enough to get a tan. It's not my idea of fun hunched up in a deckchair hour after hour.'

Mum mumbled and grumbled all the way back to the beach. I raced to the top of the cliff, ready to hurtle down.

'Tim! For goodness' sake! Do you want to get *more* sand in that eye? Use the path!'

I stopped listening to Mum. I saw who else was on the beach. Kelly and Kelly's mum and Kelly's mum's boyfriend Dave and Kelly's little brother Dean and Kelly's baby brother Keanu.

'Look who's here, Mum!' I said, and I charged down the sandy slope, too impatient to bother with the path.

Kelly's mum was sitting in my mum's deckchair

beside Dad. Kelly's mum's boyfriend Dave was sitting on the sand with baby Keanu on his lap. Dean was scrunched up in Keanu's buggy pretending to be a baby. Kelly and Biscuits were sitting on a beach towel, Kelly wriggling and pushing, Biscuits refusing to budge. They all had ice-creams. I felt a little left out – and then as I slid nearer I saw Kelly was holding an ice-cream in each hand.

'Hey, Tim! Is your eye better? I was worried when your dad told us. I've saved you an ice-cream anyway,' Kelly shouted. 'Better come quick. Biscuits has been after it!'

'Well, it's all started to melt,' said Biscuits.

'You're an old greedy-guts, you are,' said Kelly, bounding forward to meet me.

She nudged Biscuits a bit in the process. He dropped his own ice-cream in the sand. It was nearly finished anyway, but he gave an immense howl of protest.

I suggested he had half of my ice-cream to make up. I could see it might be a bit difficult to keep things peaceful between Biscuits and Kelly. I liked Biscuits ever so much and I sort of liked Kelly a lot too. I couldn't see why they didn't seem to like each other much.

Mum didn't look at all pleased when she arrived on the beach. She glared at me.

'I told you *not* to go down the sandy way, Tim,' she

hissed. Then she smiled, though her lips were very thin and showing too much teeth. 'Well, this is a lovely surprise.'

'Oh, we can't keep our Kelly away from your Tim,' Kelly's mum laughed, still sprawling in Mum's deckchair, her skirt pulled up so she showed a lot of long brown leg.

Mum's smile got even thinner as she sat down heavily on the sand.

'Oh don't sit down! I want you to come with me,' said Kelly's mum. She leapt up and started hopping around, brushing the sand off her feet and stuffing them into strappy little sandals. 'There's meant to be a huge great market this morning in a field the other side of Abercoch. I've been trying to get your old man and mine interested, but you know what men are like when it comes to shopping. But you'll come, won't you?'

'There you are, Mum! You can go shopping after all,' I said, trying to squeeze in between Kelly and Biscuits. It was a terrible squash.

Mum got a bit dithery, but eventually agreed.

'Come along then, children,' she said.

'Oh, we won't take the *kids*. They'll be a terrible bore. The boys hate shopping.'

'Tim enjoys it,' said Mum. 'And I daresay Biscuits will come if there's any food in the offing.'

'Me?' said Biscuits.

'No, let them play on the beach and have fun. The boys might behave themselves but my Kelly will be on and on at me to buy her everything.'

'Me?' said Kelly.

'And Dean *won't* hold my hand and I'm always on pins in case I lose him – and the baby's so grizzly with his teething he's driving me round the bend. No, we'll leave the kids with the men.'

'Oh, I don't think we could do that,' said Mum. 'They'd let them run wild.'

'I daresay!' said Kelly's mum. She linked her arm through my mum's. 'They can have fun and we'll have fun too. Come on. I insist!'

So Mum went off with Kelly's mum. As soon as she started picking her way across the sand Biscuits said, 'Hooray!'

And so did Kelly. So I did too.

'Now, what are we going to do?' said Kelly. 'Let's explore those rocks over there, right?'

'OK. There might be shrimps,' I said.

'The sort you can eat?' said Biscuits.

'You'd eat *any* sort,' said Kelly scornfully. 'You are a pig, Biscuits. And you've got ice-cream all round your mouth.'

'*You've* got your breakfast orange juice all round yours,' said Biscuits.

 137

'Don't be stupid. It's lipstick. My mum's Coral Peach. Honestly!' said Kelly, tossing her pony-tail. 'Come on, Tim.'

I dithered between them. I *wished* they felt more friendly towards each other.

'Where are you three off to?' said Dad.

'We're just going to climb about on those rocks,' said Kelly, giving him a dazzling smile.

'Good idea,' said Dad.

'Me too, me too, me too,' said Dean, trying to climb out of the baby buggy. He tripped over the safety strap and sprawled headlong in the sand.

'Quick!' said Kelly. 'We don't want to get lumbered with him.'

She ran. I ran too. And Biscuits ran, awkwardly, because he'd only had time to put one trainer on.

We got to the rocks at the edge of the beach and started climbing up them. It was quite hard, with big gaps in between the rocks, but I was desperate to show Kelly I could do it. At least I had my trainers on. Biscuits winced and whimpered at every second step.

'You're such a *wimp*, Biscuits,' said Kelly. 'Look, I haven't got shoes on either, have I, but I'm not making a fuss.'

The soles of Kelly's feet were hard and dark and leathery, almost as if she had shoes built into her skin.

138

Biscuits' feet were pale pink and as smooth as satin cushions. Kelly wasn't really being fair.

'*Ouch!*' said Biscuits, stepping on a really spiky rock with his bare foot.

'Try treading on the seaweedy parts, it'll be softer,' I suggested.

It was bad advice. The seaweed was like an oiled slide. Biscuits stepped, slipped, screamed. His arms went up. His legs went up too. He landed very heavily indeed on his bottom.

I felt so sorry for him. But he also looked so funny. Kelly shrieked with laughter. I struggled to stay straight-faced. But Biscuits looked so *comical* sitting in the seaweed. I snorted and then I couldn't stop. I laughed too.

'Oh ha ha ha ha,' said Biscuits sourly.

'I'm sorry, Biscuits,' I spluttered. 'Oh dear, have you hurt yourself?'

'Probably,' said Biscuits, standing up gingerly.

'Are your legs all right? You haven't broken anything?' I asked, patting and prodding him.

Kelly was still laughing.

'Kelly!' I said.

'Look at his shorts! It looks as if he's wet himself!' said Kelly.

'Don't be mean,' I said – but my voice shook. I was very nearly laughing again. The seaweed was very wet

 139

and slimy. Biscuits' shorts were wet in the very worst places.

Biscuits stood dripping in his damp shorts. He took Dog Hog out of his pocket and dabbed him dry. Poor Dog Hog had endured several salt-water baths this holiday.

'You could change into your swimming trunks,' I suggested.

Biscuits didn't bother to reply. He gave Dog Hog one last squeeze and then stuffed him back in his sodden pocket. He turned with as much dignity as he could muster, very nearly slipped over again, wobbled dangerously, and then started his descent.

'Oh dear,' I said, watching Biscuits plod across the beach. 'Poor Biscuits. Do you think I should go after him?'

'No! Leave him be. He'll go and eat a biscuit or two – or three or four or five or six – and cheer himself up. It's nice to be without him for a bit. He's worse than our Dean for tagging on when he's not wanted,' said Kelly, climbing again.

'*I* want Biscuits around,' I said.

'Well *I* don't,' said Kelly, as if that settled it. 'Come on, Tim, let's get to the top.'

She hauled me up and up and up. It was getting uncomfortably high.

'Hang on. Look, here's a little rockpool. What's this blobby red thing? I think it's a sea anemone.'

'Mmm,' said Kelly, clearly not interested. She pulled at a few mussels clinging to the rock.

'Don't dislodge them!'

'Are they oysters?' Kelly asked. 'I could do with a pearl to ring the changes with my diamond.'

'Oysters!' I said, sighing. 'Oysters are *completely* different, and they're way down on the sea bed. You have to dive for them.'

'Theresa can dive for them then,' said Kelly, getting her old troll doll out of the pocket of her sweatshirt.

I wished my Walter Bear was little enough to fit in a pocket. Kelly and Biscuits were so lucky to have mascots so discreetly small. I'd need a pocket the size of a shopping bag to accommodate Walter.

Kelly ripped Theresa's dress off and made her dive down into the pool.

'Wheee! She likes it, see. She's a great swimmer. Find me some oysters, please, I want some pearls.'

'You don't get pearls in every oyster. They're very rare. Though of course you can farm oysters and have cultivated pearls—'

'Tim,' Kelly interrupted. 'Do you want to be a school teacher when you grow up?'

'Why?'

'Because you don't half *act* like one sometimes.'

'Oh,' I said.

'Oooooooooh!' said Kelly.

141

I blinked at her. I wondered if she was mocking me. Or playing the fool with Theresa? She scooped her troll out of the little pool and was holding her at arm's length.

'Help! Look what's in her *hair*!' Kelly yelled.

I looked. Then I laughed.

'Oh Kelly. It's just a weeny little crab. Theresa used her hair like a fishing net.'

'Get it *off* her. She doesn't like it,' Kelly said urgently, waggling Theresa frantically.

'Hold her still then. Come here.' I held the little wet troll doll and gently untangled the tiny crab from her long purple locks.

'*Yuck!*' said Kelly, snatching Theresa back and combing her hair with her fingers. 'Poor poor *poor* Theresa – under mega-attack from a sea monster!'

'It's only a baby crab, Kelly. Nothing to be scared of,' I said, letting the crab scuttle up my arm.

'*I'm* not afraid of it. Theresa is. It practically bit her head off. Ugh, put it back in the water.'

I popped the little crab back into his swimming pool. He paddled out of sight, probably very relieved.

'That's it, you go back to Mummy Crab,' I said.

'*Mummy?*' said Kelly.

She started climbing higher very quickly. I climbed too. I was getting the knack of it now and leapt from rock to rock almost as if I were Super-Tim himself. I felt great (though a bit guilty about Biscuits).

'Wow!' said Kelly, from up above. 'There's an even better beach the other side of these rocks. A little cove.'

It took me a minute or two to get up to the top. Then I saw the beach for myself. It was fantastic, a miniature bay of soft white sand circled by tall cliffs.

'Maybe no one's ever spotted it before,' said Kelly. 'It looks like you can only reach it by going over the rocks from our beach. Hey, let's get right down there and make it *ours*. We can call it Kelly-and-Tim beach. Come on!'

'Well. Hadn't we better get Biscuits too?'

'No!'

'It's not really fair if we go off without him.'

'He's the one that went off, not us.'

'Yes, but—'

'Look, if we go all the way back to get him and then have to climb back all over the rocks, it'll take for ever. Let's just slip down to the beach and claim it – and *then* we'll go back and make friends with him if we must, OK?'

'OK,' I said.

'Great,' said Kelly. She was immediately off like a mountain goat down the other side of the rocks to the perfect private beach.

'Kelly, *wait*. I can't go as fast. And it's all difficult and slippery. Suppose we can't get back up?'

 143

'Of course we'll be able to,' Kelly said, leaping a long way down.

She landed lightly on a flat rock, but it wasn't wedged securely. It wobbled. Kelly wobbled too, but leapt again before she fell. She landed on another lower rock, safely – but only just.

'Kelly! Do be careful. If you slip and break your leg how could I possibly carry you all the way back?' I protested.

'You're such a worryguts, Tim. I'm not *going* to slip,' Kelly shouted.

She leapt.

She landed.

She slipped – and fell.

I screamed.

She grabbed another rock, hung there, stretched one leg to another rock, steadied herself, edged downwards, and stood properly on her two tough feet.

'Kelly! Are you OK?'

'I'm fine.'

'I thought you were going to fall all the way down.'

'I didn't fall at all. I slid that bit on purpose,' Kelly insisted.

But when we both got down to the soft sand I saw a great gash on Kelly's leg.

'You're bleeding!'

'It's nothing,' said Kelly, dabbing her leg impatiently.

 144

'Hey, isn't this beach fantastic? Aren't you pleased I discovered it for you?'

'It's a deep cut, Kelly. You must clean it.'

'Oh Tim, stop fussing. I'm always getting cuts. They're usually far far worse than that. I climbed over a wall with all this broken glass stuck on top once. Look!' Kelly lifted her T-shirt and showed a zig-zag scar across her tummy.

'Gosh!' I said, very impressed.

'I used to kid the guys in my class it was like a zip and I could shove my hand straight into my stomach.'

'You couldn't, could you?'

'No!'

'Well anyway, you ought to go paddling. The sea's salty. It's very healing. My dad had a boil on his bottom once, and he sat in a basin of salty water.'

Kelly snorted with laughter. So did I. We laughed so much we nearly fell over on the sand.

'What a place to have a boil!' said Kelly. 'OK, OK. I'll paddle, just to keep you happy.'

We both paddled. Kelly winced a bit as the water washed over her leg but she didn't complain.

'You're ever so brave, Kelly,' I said.

Kelly beamed at me. A wave splashed high and she jumped to stop her shorts getting wet. Soon we were both holding hands and jumping every wave. We got wet after all but it didn't really matter. Little droplets

 145

of water on my eyelashes made me see rainbows everywhere.

'This is our beach, right? We're the only ones who can come here,' said Kelly. 'Let's stake it out as *ours*.'

She searched the sands until she found a big stick. She went near the water's edge where the sand was firm and wrote a message in spiky capital letters.

KELLY-AND-TIM BEACH. PRIVATE. KEEP OUT.

Then she bent over and started drawing a big heart. Well, it was meant to be a heart but it went a bit wobbly and lop-sided. She wrote K L T inside.

'What's it say?' I said. 'Klut? Klot?'

'You're the clot,' said Kelly, pink from bending over. 'It says Kelly Loves Tim. Right?'

'Oh. Right,' I said.

'*Well?*' said Kelly. She held out the stick.

Obediently I drew my own heart and put T L K inside.

'Right!' said Kelly. She came up very close.

'Shut your eyes!' she commanded.

I did as I was told. I felt this quick dab on my cheek. I *think* she kissed me. But when I opened my eyes she'd already darted right across the sand towards the rocks.

Tim's diary

This was the most <u>terrifying</u> day of my life. Really. I am not exaggerating. Honest. Biscuits almost betrayed me.

I was helplessly trapped and in dreadful danger. And then the Deadly Fiendish Enemy ambushed me. He very, very nearly injured me grievously. <u>Practically murdered me.</u>

My hand is still shaking as I write this.

I am sick of adventures.

This has been the worst yet.

Biscuits' diary

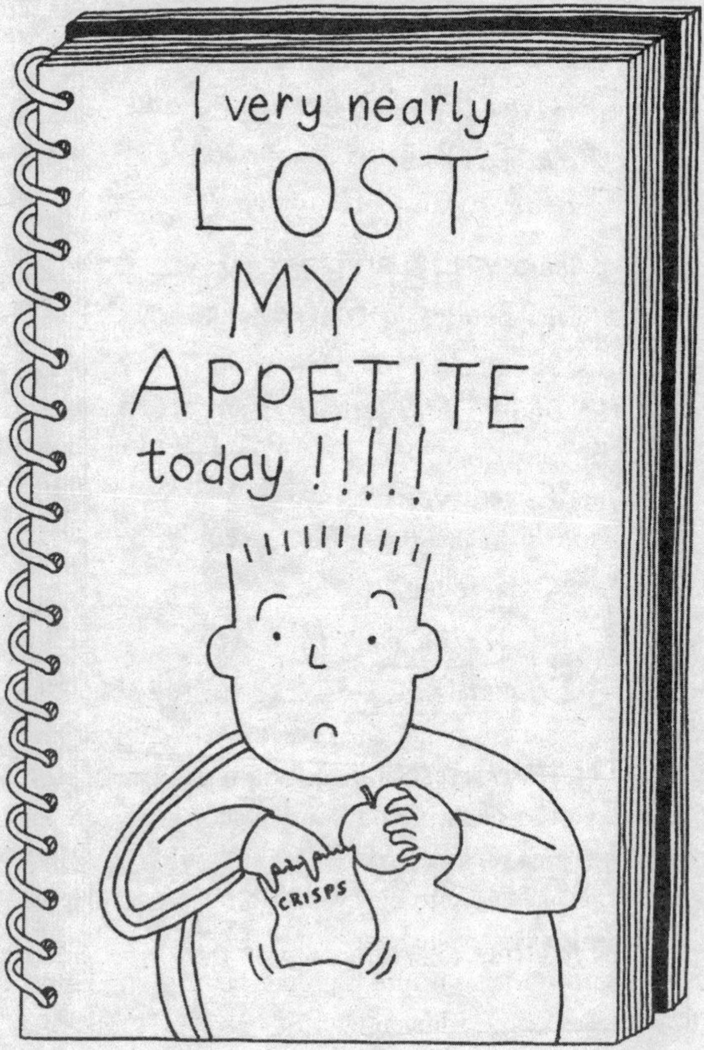

✪ CHAPTER SIX ✪

Biscuits was very huffy indeed when Kelly and I climbed back onto the ordinary beach. I kept telling him this and telling him that but he wouldn't answer. I tried cracking some of our extra-funny jokes but he wouldn't even smile.

Kelly absolutely fell about laughing and said, 'Oh Tim, you are *funny*.'

Biscuits became even less friendly. He chatted to Kelly's little brother Dean instead. He helped him finish a giant tube of Smarties and in return he built Dean a little boat in the sand just big enough for him to sit in. He encouraged Dean to hold the empty Smarties packet up to his eye like a telescope.

It was a very *basic* boat.

'Shall we make it into a proper boat?' I suggested. 'What sort of boat do you want it to be? Is it a rowing boat or a sailing boat or maybe a big ocean-going liner?'

'I bet you've done a special project on blooming boats,' said Biscuits. 'It's just a little sand boat for Dean, OK?'

'Yeah. It's my boat, not your boat,' said Dean.

'Leave the little boys with their soppy boats and come and swim, Tim,' said Kelly, trying to pull me away.

I dithered, desperate to keep in with both Biscuits and Kelly. Eventually we all went in for a swim. Kelly's mum's boyfriend Dave even dangled Keanu in up to his ankles.

Kelly was a seriously super swimmer, much better than Biscuits or me. She showed off rather a lot, and kept challenging us to races. She won every time. Biscuits stopped competing. He lay on his back and practised spouting like a whale. I tried too but I couldn't get the knack of spouting. The water went in instead of out and I had a major choking fit. I retreated to the shallows after that and hung around, getting a bit shivery.

I was even more shivery by the time we'd all got out and got dressed.

'We all need to run about and get warm,' said Dad. 'I know. French cricket!'

But luckily my mum and Kelly's mum came back from their trip to the market just then and they'd bought *hot dogs*. They were only lukewarm dogs actually, but they still tasted great, and it stopped Dad banging on about cricket. Even Biscuits cheered up a little – but he looked anxious after he'd eaten his hot dog in three great big bites.

'That's not *lunch*, is it?' he said.

Mum sighed. 'You and your stomach, Biscuits,' she said. But she was in a very good mood after her trip out. She had lots of carrier bags full of shoes and tops and trousers and underwear. She also had *another* carrier full of food.

'Picnic,' she said.

'Is it for us lot too?' said Kelly.

'No Kelly, you know we said we'd find a nice pub with a garden,' said Kelly's mum, trying a new T-shirt on Dave. It had a rude message on it. She'd bought him some new underpants too with an even *ruder* message.

Kelly's mum and Kelly's mum's boyfriend Dave tried to get my mum and dad to go to the pub too. My mum said they were welcome to share our picnic on the beach if they wanted. She seemed much friendlier with Kelly's mum now – though she frowned at Kelly's mum's boyfriend Dave's new naughty underpants.

'There might not be enough picnic to go round,' said Biscuits.

He was very relieved when Kelly's mum and Kelly's mum's boyfriend Dave and Kelly herself and

Dean and Keanu all went off to the pub while we stayed on the beach. Kelly wanted to go to the pub for pizza and chips but she was very cross to leave us behind. Well . . . *me*.

'I can come back to see Tim after lunch, can't I?' she said.

'We'll see, pet. We might go on a fishing trip or something,' said Kelly's mum's boyfriend Dave.

'Well, can't Tim come too?' said Kelly.

'He doesn't like fishing,' said Biscuits.

Kelly pulled a face and made a fuss. We could still hear her complaining and arguing halfway down the beach.

'That kiddie isn't half a little madam,' said Mum, dealing out paper plates and little packs of sandwiches.

'She's a sparky little thing though. A cracking swimmer,' said Dad.

'I like her,' I said.

'I don't,' said Biscuits.

We didn't say much else while we ate our picnic lunch. It was banana sandwiches. I particularly like banana sandwiches but I gave half of mine to Biscuits. And my sausage roll. And most of my crisps too.

'You're trying to bribe me to be friends,' said Biscuits.

'Yes,' I said.

'Well. It's working,' said Biscuits.

'Oh Biscuits! Are we really friends again? Oh *great*!'

'I didn't really break friends. *You* were the one who laughed at me and went off with Kelly.'

'I didn't really mean to,' I said.

'I don't know what you *see* in her,' said Biscuits.

'I don't either,' I said. 'But I do like her. I like you too! I wish you and Kelly would be friends.'

'You've got to be joking!' said Biscuits. 'What were you two *doing* all that time over the rocks?'

'Oh. Just exploring. There's this little cove.'

'Is it good there? Any pirate caves?'

'I don't really know. We didn't find any.'

'*We* could find some,' said Biscuits, getting up.

'What, now?'

'Yep. Come on. *We'll* go and explore.' Biscuits was tying up the laces on his trainers. 'In the right foot gear this time.' He grabbed his spade. 'Here's my trusty bashing stick in case we encounter any wild animals – or boys.'

'I think you might find it an awful bore getting over all the rocks,' I said.

I didn't know what to do. I so badly wanted Biscuits to stay friends with me. But I wasn't sure I should let him come to Tim-and-Kelly beach. Of course it wasn't *really* our private place. I wouldn't really mind sharing it with Biscuits – but I knew *Kelly* would!

Mum didn't like the idea much either.

 153

'I don't want you clambering over those rocks out of sight. I want you to play here on this beach where we can keep an eye on you.'

'Look, we're not *babies*,' said Biscuits. 'And Tim and Kelly went over the rocks this morning.'

'That was nothing to do with me,' said Mum, glaring at Dad.

'It's not fair if I can't go and explore too,' said Biscuits.

'Hey, *I'll* go with the boys,' said Dad.

So Dad and Biscuits and I set off over the rocks. I just hoped like anything Kelly wouldn't find out. I felt pretty anxious when we got to the top of the rocks because I suddenly remembered the messages we'd left in the sand. There might be some serious teasing.

But the tide had come in. Like a kindly mum with a flannel, the sea had washed the sand clean of all marks.

'Wow! It's a super beach,' said Biscuits.

'We can build a castle now the sand's still wet,' I said.

'You and your castles,' said Biscuits. 'You're like one of them Egyptians wanting a pyramid built, only you haven't got millions of slaves, you've just got me. OK then. Let's get cracking.'

There was just one problem. We only had one spade with us.

'Feel free to use mine, Tim,' said Biscuits, after he'd had three feeble little digs and started a sandcastle the size of a pygmy molehill. Share and share alike.' He handed the spade over with a happy sigh and sat on a rock.

I had a go. A long go. But the sand still wasn't *obedient* enough. I had this splendid vision of a castle in my head but it kept blurring and collapsing in the actual sand.

'Let's dig down and make a big hole instead,' I said, giving up.

I started digging. And digging and digging and digging.

Then Dad took a turn. He got very red in the face. He breathed very heavily. Then he straightened up, rubbing his back.

'I'll have to stop, it's doing my back in. I'm going back to Mum. I'll tell her it's perfectly safe for you two boys to play here. You won't go in the sea, will you?'

'No, we're going to dig and see how far down we can go,' I said.

'And you won't try and climb up the cliff?' said Dad.

'*Me?* And Biscuits?' I said. 'Leave it out, Dad.'

'Right. OK then. Have fun digging,' said Dad.

He started climbing back over the rocks, still puffing and blowing.

'It's your turn with the spade, Biscuits,' I said.

Biscuits puffed a lot too. And blew. He leant on the spade.

'Isn't it big enough now?'

'No! We're not even properly down to the dark sand yet.'

'And what's going to happen when we dig through that? We'll come out in Australia and everyone will talk like *Neighbours* and we'll have koala bears and kangaroos jumping all round us.'

'Of *course* we couldn't ever get to Australia! Don't you know anything? Honestly, Biscuits, you're so silly sometimes. We'd have to get right through the Earth's crust and you can't do that, and then you'd go into the core and that's boiling-boiling-boiling hot and—'

'And I feel boiling-boiling-boiling hot right this minute,' said Biscuits. He looked at the hole. He looked at me. 'I know. Get in it, Tim. And sit down.'

'Like this?' I did what he said, puzzled. 'Biscuits? What are you doing? Oh, don't start filling it in!'

'I'm making you a boat, right?'

'Wrong!' I said. I'd wanted to dig the biggest hole ever and see all the different layers of sand and work out how far down they went. I didn't want to mess about playing baby-boats. But I *did* want Biscuits to stay friends. So I sighed and gave up on the idea of Huge Hole.

'OK, OK, I'm in a boat,' I said, and I even helped

Biscuits heap the sand back into the hole around me. And on top of me.

'Not on my legs!'

'Yes. Go on. It's more fun like that.' He piled sand up on my lap.

'It's going to look like the boat's sinking,' I said. 'Watch the edge of that spade, Biscuits!'

'Sorry, sorry!' He put the spade down and started patting the damp sand into place.

It felt very heavy, almost uncomfortably so. I tried to shift my legs but they were already firmly stuck under the sand. I tried a violent kick and just about managed to crack the sand above my toes.

'Don't!' said Biscuits, and he got wetter sand and patted it hard.

It set like concrete.

'It's *heavy*,' I said.

'Well keep still,' said Biscuits, piling more sand on.

I tried to push it away but Biscuits took the spade and shovelled hard. My arms got covered. I was stuck.

'This isn't a boat. Not unless it's a submarine,' I said.

'Up periscope,' said Biscuits, heaping more sand right under my chin.

'Biscuits! Let me out now. I don't want to play Boats any more.'

'This isn't Playing Boats. This is the Burying Tim

game,' said Biscuits, patting and smoothing the sand harder and harder.

'Oh ha ha,' I said.

Though it didn't feel very funny. I didn't like being stuck there in the sand like that, with just my head sticking out.

Biscuits was panting with effort by now. He stopped and straightened up, wiping his wet brow. He looked at me, his head on one side.

'There! You're done now,' he said.

'Thank goodness. OK. Let me out then. Biscuits? Biscuits!'

Biscuits had started to walk away!

'Biscuits, come back!'

'What's that?' said Biscuits, turning and cupping his ear as if he couldn't quite hear me.

'Biscuits, please! Don't mess about.'

'What's the matter?'

'Don't be *silly*!'

'Ah. That's me. Silly,' said Biscuits. 'Only I'm not the one stuck up to my neck in sand. *You* are. Even though you're so clever.'

'Oh, Biscuits. Don't be like that. Look, get me *out*. It's stopped being a joke. It's not funny at all.'

'I think it's *ever* so funny. Bye, Tim!' said Biscuits, and he started a lumbering run towards the rocks.

'Biscuits! Look, you're not frightening me. It's just

your stupid joke. It's very very *boring*. So let's get it over with, right?'

Biscuits didn't seem to be listening. He started clambering over the rocks.

'I don't care a bit,' I said. 'I know you just want me to shout after you.'

He didn't turn round.

He climbed to the top and then started going down the other side. Then he dropped down. And disappeared.

'*Biscuits!*' I shouted.

A gull screamed back at me overhead. Biscuits had gone. I was all on my own.

Stuck up to my neck on a deserted beach. My heart went bang bang bang inside my chest. The gull cried again, swooping low, so that I could see its cruel yellow beak.

I shut my eyes quick.

'Go away!' I said.

It was meant to be a shout but it came out as a feeble whisper.

I waited. My eyes were getting watery behind their lids. When I dared open them tears spilled down my cheeks. I blinked hard. I didn't want Biscuits to catch me crying when he came back.

If he came back.

Of course he'd come back. Or Mum and Dad would come looking for me. Eventually.

There was nothing to cry about. The gull had flown away. It hadn't mistaken me for a juicy fish. I was fine. I couldn't come to any harm even though I was trapped.

I tried to calm myself by staring out to sea. Then I watched the waves. Was the tide coming in or out? I couldn't remember! What if the tide was coming in – rapidly? Suppose it started lapping right around my sand prison, the waves splashing over my head?

I tried kicking madly and thrusting my arms up but the sand was set too hard. It wouldn't budge. I couldn't even make the tiniest crack in it now.

'Oh Biscuits, come back!' I cried. 'Please! It's not a joke any more! I'm frightened.'

Then I heard noises up above me, from right up on the clifftop. I tried to peer round to see who was there but my neck was so packed with sand that I couldn't even swivel my head properly. I heard bumps and thumps. It sounded as if someone was climbing down the cliffs.

'Is that you, Biscuits?' I shouted.

Was this all part of his joke? I couldn't believe he could have scooted up the path to the clifftop so quickly. And surely old Biscuits wouldn't risk his neck climbing down the sheer cliff face? (Though he had been pretty good at abseiling.)

'*Biscuits?*' I yelled, as the sliding and slithering progressed downwards behind me.

Then I saw a head bob up from behind the rocks. It was munching on a chocolate bar.

'Ha ha! I *really* got you worried, didn't I?' he yelled. 'I didn't really leave you, I just hid behind the rocks.'

'Biscuits?' I said. 'Then who . . . ?'

I tried to crane round again.

I saw Biscuits stop and look behind me. His hand stopped in mid air, holding the chocolate. His mouth stayed open and empty.

I knew it was seriously bad news for Biscuits to forget to eat. My heart was banging to bursting point now. I had a sudden terrible premonition.

Someone started to give triumphant Tarzan whoops as he got nearer and nearer. I could feel my trapped skin erupting in goosebumps.

Then I heard a thump thump as two very big boots jumped onto the sand.

I saw Biscuits mouth one terrible word. Prickle-Head.

'Aha! Who have we got here?' he yelled triumphantly. 'Fun time!'

Biscuits was still standing statue-still. Then he moved. I wouldn't have blamed him for one minute if he'd clambered back over the rocks to the other beach. I think I might have done. And he could always say he was rushing off to get my dad.

But Biscuits didn't run away and really abandon me. He started running towards me, spade at the ready, all set to dig me out and rescue me.

But he didn't have time. Prickle-Head got to me first.

'What's this weird little squashy thing in the sand?' he said. 'Is it a little jellyfish?' He put his great boot right on top of my head, pressing down hard enough to hurt.

'Get off!' I said.

'Oooh! The jellyfish can talk! Yuck, it really *is* a jellyfish, there's slime and snot all over its face.'

I sniffed desperately.

'Oh my, it's not a jellyfish at all, it's the little Mummy's boy. What's happened to its weedy wimpy little body then? Someone's chopped its head off. Well, it's no use to anyone. Might as well use it as a football, eh?' He took his boot off my head and took aim.

'Don't you dare kick him!' Biscuits yelled, and he started whirling the spade in a threatening manner.

But Prickle-Head was bigger and quicker. He dodged, pushed and grabbed.

Biscuits ended up on his bottom.

Prickle-Head ended up with the spade.

'Aha! It's *my* turn to play sandcastles now,' said Prickle-Head. 'Here's a nice castle. Ready-made, couldn't be better. Hey, look at my castle, Rick.'

There was another thump on the sand behind me. Prickle-Head had reinforcements.

Pinch-Face came running into my view. He laughed and aimed a kick at my head. He missed – but only just. I tried to dodge and jarred all down my back.

'Yeah, I don't like that wet blobby bit on top of the castle. Spoils it, doesn't it? So shall I pat it smooth, eh?' Prickle-Head held the spade high and then brought it down hard and fast.

I screamed.

Biscuits leapt up and tried to rugby tackle Prickle-Head. The spade swung and landed with a loud bang on the tightly-packed sand.

'Get *off*, Fatboy,' said Prickle-Head, and he punched Biscuits in the stomach.

Biscuits made a sad little 'oooof ' sound, and sank into the sand like a burst balloon.

'Now, let's play Hit the Head,' said Prickle-Head, grabbing the spade again.

'Sounds like fun, Boss,' said Pinch-Face.

'Look, if you really hit me with that you could easily *kill* me,' I said desperately.

'Ooooh! Mummy's boy is getting really scared now. I bet he's wetting his little panties,' said Prickle-Head.

'*Why* do you want to be so hateful? I haven't done anything to you,' I said, snuffling hard.

'It's fun,' said Prickle-Head. 'Right. I'll take aim.' He raised the spade high above my head. 'And then I'm going to go WHACK!'

'Hey, Boss,' said Pinch-Face. 'You're not *really* going to?'

'What? Are you chicken or something?'

'Of course not. It's just like the cissy said. You could really smash his head in,' Pinch-Face said. 'You're just kidding, aren't you?'

'Am I?' said Prickle-Head. 'You just wait and see. Right. One, two, three . . .'

He waved the spade above his head, his face contorted with effort. I stared up into his eyes. I didn't know if he was really going to do it or not. Maybe he didn't even know either.

'Please don't!' I begged.

But that just made him grin.

'Ready steady *GO*!'

'Hey! You! Stop that! Get away from my boy!'

It was Dad, over at the rocks, scrambling down, the other spade in his hand.

Prickle-Head waved the spade in mid-air.

'Hey, Boss, we'd better scarper,' said Pinch-Face.

He started running.

Prickle-Head whirled the spade one last time and then threw it as far as he could. Then he ran too.

'Oh, Tim!' Biscuits gasped, still rolled up in a ball clutching his stomach. 'Are you all right?'

'Oh, Biscuits!' I said. 'Are *you* all right?'

We both felt very wrong indeed. I cried a bit. And

so did Biscuits. And then Dad got to us and dug me out, and rubbed Biscuits' tummy, and gave us both a big hug.

'I couldn't believe my eyes!' he said. 'Thank goodness I decided to bring you the other spade. How dare those boys behave like that!' He waved his fist at Prickle-Head and Pinch-Face who were scrambling up the cliff.

'You stupid bullying little thugs! And you're mad to be climbing that cliff. You'll break your necks – and it'll serve you right.'

Prickle-Head yelled a very rude word at Dad.

'Just wait till I find out exactly who that lad is,' said Dad. 'I've a good mind to go to the local police. That wasn't childish rough play – that was atrocious bullying. Imagine burying you in the sand like that, Tim! How did he do it? Didn't you struggle?'

I hesitated.

'Mm. *I* actually buried Tim in the sand,' said Biscuits.

'*You* did, Biscuits?' said Dad. 'Good Heavens! Why? Tim's your friend.'

'I know. It was just a silly joke. I wasn't really going to leave him like that. I just hid for a minute. But then Prickle-Head came down the cliffs—'

'Biscuits tried to stop him,' I said. 'He was very brave.'

 165

'It was still my fault you were stuck there and couldn't run away from him,' said Biscuits. 'What's your mum going to say when she finds out?'

We all three thought about Mum.

'Ah,' said Dad. 'Well. Seeing as there's no lasting harm done . . . shall us men keep quiet about it? We don't want to worry your mum, Tim. You know what she's like.'

'Yes,' I said.

'*Yes!*' said Biscuits.

'So, if we dust you both down, and mop you up a bit, Mum won't need to know. But I'm still in two minds whether to go to the police or not. Or if I could track down where the boy is staying I could have a serious word with his father.'

We saw Prickle-Head that evening when we went to a fun fair with Kelly and Kelly's mum and Kelly's mum's boyfriend Dave and Kelly's little brother Dean and Kelly's baby brother Keanu.

Prickle-Head was there with *his* mum and his dad and several pricklet brothers and sisters. They all looked almost as fierce and frightening as their big brother Prickle-Head. His *mum* looked fierce and frightening too. She was shouting at the older children. Then Prickle-Head's dad whacked them hard about the head. He gave Prickle-Head a couple of extra smacks. Prickle-Head's dad looked far far far fiercer and more frightening than Prickle-Head.

Dad decided that he wouldn't have a serious word with him after all.

Wow.

And **Wow** again.

WOW
WOW
WOW!!!

I have had my biggest adventure yet!

Biscuits' diary

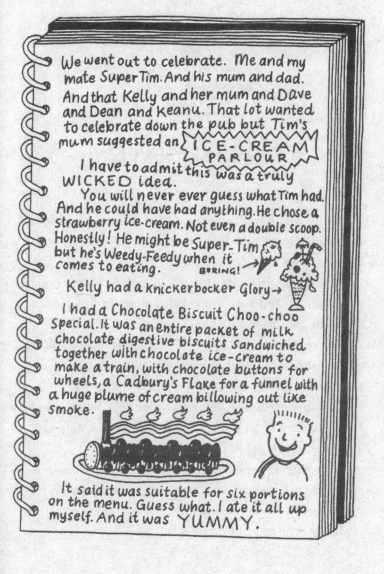

We went out to celebrate. Me and my mate Super Tim. And his mum and dad. And that Kelly and her mum and Dave and Dean and Keanu. That lot wanted to celebrate down the pub but Tim's mum suggested an ICE-CREAM PARLOUR

I have to admit this was a truly WICKED idea.

You will never ever guess what Tim had. And he could have had anything. He chose a strawberry ice-cream. Not even a double scoop. Honestly! He might be Super-Tim but he's Weedy-Feedy when it comes to eating. BORING!

Kelly had a knickerbocker Glory →

I had a Chocolate Biscuit Choo-choo Special. It was an entire packet of milk chocolate digestive biscuits sandwiched together with chocolate ice-cream to make a train, with chocolate buttons for wheels, a Cadbury's Flake for a funnel with a huge plume of cream billowing out like smoke.

It said it was suitable for six portions on the menu. Guess what. I ate it all up myself. And it was YUMMY.

✮ CHAPTER SEVEN ✮

Kelly was barely talking to me. Biscuits had told her about our last desperate encounter with Prickle-Head.

'You took Biscuits to our beach?' Kelly cried indignantly. 'You rat. You total traitorous flea-ridden slimy-tailed rotten rat!'

She kept repeating this, with yet more ratty embellishments, all the while we told her about our narrow escape.

'Do shut it, Kelly. You don't own the beach,' said Biscuits. 'Don't you realize, I got beaten to a pulp and Tim practically got his head bashed in.'

'The way Prickle-Head was holding the spade it could have sliced off the top of my head just like a boiled egg!' I said dramatically.

Kelly refused to be impressed.

170

'If I'd caught you there with Biscuits I'd have jumped up and down on your head myself,' she said darkly.

She waved Theresa Troll in the air and hit me hard before I had time to duck. It was surprising how much a plastic troll could hurt.

'*Ouch!*' I said, reeling. I had to try very very hard not to cry.

'Serves you right,' said Kelly. 'Just be glad Theresa's not a sharp spade. I'm not like this stupid Prickle-Head you keep going on about. I don't miss when I take aim.'

She stalked off, her pony-tail switching furiously right and left.

'Wow!' said Biscuits. 'Old Killer-Kelly, eh? I dropped you in it there all right, didn't I, Super-Tim?'

'Too right, Biscuits-Boy,' I said, rubbing my head ruefully.

I sighed. At least I was back being friends with Biscuits. I hoped that Kelly might have got over her mega-huff by tomorrow. I so wanted us *all* to be friends.

'What's up, dear?' said Mum, coming and putting her arm round me. 'You're looking a bit peaky. How's your poor old eye? It's not still smarting, is it? It looks a bit watery.'

'It's fine, Mum, really,' I said.

'It's silly, everyone thinks sandy beaches are so safe – and yet they can cause all sorts of problems,' said Mum.

 171

'I know,' I said. I wondered what Mum would say if she knew of my problems in the sand with Prickle-Head.

'I'd be happy to give the beach a miss tomorrow,' said Mum, keeping her voice down. 'We could go for a car trip, maybe explore another castle. You'd like that, wouldn't you, Tim? And Biscuits will go along with that so long as we feed him every five minutes.' Mum sniffed.

'You bet I will,' said Biscuits, who had sharp ears.

'So it's all settled,' said Mum. 'We'll go on a car trip, just the four of us.'

'What's that?' said Dad, coming over. 'Not tomorrow. It's the Caravan Site Carnival Day and we've all been invited, remember?'

'Oh yes,' said Mum. 'But Tim and Biscuits want to go for a car ride, don't you boys?'

'I'd sooner go to a carnival,' said Biscuits. I saw the dreamy look in his eyes. Carnivals meant ice-creams and candy floss and hot dogs.

'What about you, Tim?' said Mum.

I hesitated. I hated to upset her. But if I didn't go to this Carnival Day I knew I'd upset Kelly even more. I rubbed the sore place on my forehead where Theresa Troll had clouted me.

'I'd like to go to the Carnival Day too,' I said.

It was a BIG mistake.

The moment we got to the caravan site and saw the ropes and flags set out across the beach I realized something terrible.

There were going to be sports.

I am the least sporty boy ever.

'Great!' said Dad, reading the poster. 'There's going to be all sorts of races. Sprinting, relay, three-legged, sack race, egg and spoon. You boys must have a go.'

'It'll be just for people staying at the caravan site,' I said quickly. 'We can't enter, it wouldn't be fair.'

'Don't be such a wimp, Tim,' Dad said sharply. 'Of course you can enter.'

'But I don't want to!' I said.

'Nor do I, actually,' said Biscuits loyally.

'There! We'd have all been much better off if we'd gone for a car ride,' said Mum. 'In fact, why don't we still go? This carnival doesn't look very exciting. There aren't any craft or bric-a-brac stalls, and the tombola prizes don't look much cop. There aren't even many food stalls.'

'Yes, let's go for a car ride,' said Biscuits.

Dad looked exasperated.

'But all Kelly's family are expecting us.'

'I think we've seen a little too much of Kelly's family this holiday,' Mum muttered.

'Yes, I like it best when it's just us,' said Biscuits.

Mum blinked at Biscuits – and then offered him a piece of chocolate out of her handbag to cement their new alliance.

'Tim, you want to see Kelly, don't you?' said Dad.

I dithered. Perhaps there wasn't much point seeing Kelly at the moment, seeing as she wasn't speaking to me. It would be a bit like watching telly with the sound turned down.

'Well . . .'

I heard someone shouting through a megaphone.

'Come and enter for the first race of the day, folks!'

'I want to go on a car trip,' I said.

Mum smiled.

Biscuits smiled.

Dad frowned. But it was three against one so we turned round and started walking away from the caravan site.

'Hey, Tim! TIM! TIM!!'

It was Kelly. She was speaking to me again. She didn't need a megaphone. She had her volume turned right up to maximum force.

'Pretend you haven't heard her,' said Biscuits.

It was not a sensible suggestion. People covered their ears the length of the Welsh coast and said 'That's Kelly!' Cattle in the meadows were mooing 'That's Kelly!' Sheep up in the mountains were baaing 'That's Kelly!' Dolphins and whales way out in the ocean were spouting 'That's Kelly!' Little green men in flying saucers were twitching their antennae and mumbling in Martian 'That's Kelly!'

I turned. We all turned.

Kelly came charging up to us.

'Where are you *going*? The carnival's over on the clifftop. Come on, they've just announced the first race. It's the under-five fifty-steps toddle and our Dean's going to walk it, you watch!'

'I'm sure he will, dear. But we were actually wondering whether to give all these races a miss,' said Mum.

'You can't. I've entered all of you,' said Kelly.

'What?' I said.

'You're doing the three-legged race with me, Tim. Come *on* in case it's next,' Kelly commanded.

'That's it, Kelly, you get this lazy lot organized,' said Dad.

'I've entered you in the dads' race. And there's a knobbly knees contest too. You're down for that and all,' said Kelly.

'Knobbly knees!' said Dad, looking down his shorts at his legs. 'I haven't *got* knobbly knees, young woman.'

'Well, there's a hairiest leg contest too. Would you sooner go in for that?' said Kelly.

'Cheek!' said Dad.

'I told you those shorts were a mistake,' said Mum, sniggering. 'It'll be funny if you win!'

 175

'You might win too,' said Kelly, smiling at her.

Mum blinked. 'Kelly,' she said, very slowly and ominously. 'What have you entered me for?'

'Well, the mums' race, of course. And the Fabulous Forty-Plus Beauty Contest.'

Mum snorted. Dad snorted too.

'Kelly!' said Mum. 'I am *not* forty-plus.'

'Oh well, never mind,' said Kelly. 'You've a good chance of winning it then, haven't you? Come on, we must get a move on or we'll miss Dean's race.'

So we got a move on.

You simply can't argue with Kelly. She's like a steamroller.

'I shall go in for the sack race,' Biscuits muttered. 'And I shall try hard to barge into Kelly. And I shall knock her over. And jump on her. Hard.'

But I could tell his heart wasn't in it. Biscuits was twice Kelly's fighting weight but he knew he'd never get the better of her.

He cheered up a little watching Dean's race. He had got quite matey with him during their boat-building session. Dean wasn't the oldest and he wasn't the biggest under-five by any means but it was obvious he was taking the race very seriously. Most of the kids were fidgeting or talking or whimpering or waving at their mums as they lined up at the starting post on the grass. One or two were facing the wrong way. They had to be turned round quickly or they might have gone hurtling towards the cliff edge and hurled themselves over the top like lemmings. But Dean was clearly concentrating, his teeth gritted, his fists clenched. When someone shouted 'One two three – go!' Dean was off like a shot, charging along, his elbows flapping like little wings. One big kid tripped over just in front of him. Dean ran straight over him, never pausing.

'That's it, our Dean!' Kelly yelled.

'Go for it, Dean!' Biscuits yelled.

'Come on, Dean!' Kelly's mum yelled, standing just beyond the finishing post, holding out her arms to him.

Dean won.

Kelly and Kelly's mum and Kelly's mum's boyfriend Dave and my mum and my dad and Biscuits and me all cheered. Baby Keanu, perched up on Dave's shoulders, gave a cheery sort of chirp.

Dean was given a winner's badge and a little bar of chocolate.

'Wow!' said Biscuits. 'I didn't know they gave you *chocolate*. Hey Dean, are you going in for the three-legged race? How's about you teaming up with me, eh?'

Dean was pleased to be partners with his new pal Biscuits but their pairing wasn't very successful. Dean was little but ran very fast. Biscuits was big but ran very slowly. They fell over. They fell over again.

And again. And then Biscuits tried picking Dean up and carrying him, still with their legs tied together. And then they fell over again because they were laughing so much. Luckily Biscuits was so well padded he didn't hurt himself at all and Dean always managed to land on top of Biscuits so it was just like bouncing on a huge well-stuffed sofa.

Kelly and I didn't do much better.

My heart sank as she tied our legs together with her mum's scarf. She did it so tightly she cut off all the blood supply to my foot. She looked very determined. Kelly liked to win.

I would have liked to win too. But I knew we didn't have a chance.

I tried hard to get ready, get steady and go.

'Run!' Kelly commanded.

I ran. She ran. But not together.

We tripped over. It hurt rather a lot. I wondered if I ought to stay lying there on the grass.

'Get up!' Kelly squealed.

I decided to get up. I was barely on my feet before Kelly tore off again. I staggered along beside her for three or four paces, and then tripped again.

'Oh Tim, you're so *useless*!' Kelly yelled.

I agreed with her meekly.

'Look, shut up and get up,' Kelly said sharply.

I tried to do as I was told. It didn't work.

We were last in the three-legged race. We didn't actually finish. Kelly tore the scarf off our legs and stormed off. I was left to limp the rest of the way to the finishing post by myself with everyone laughing at me. I saw Kelly's mum and Kelly's mum's boyfriend Dave pretending not to have noticed. I saw Mum's face. I saw *Dad*. I felt so awful. Then I heard another loud braying laugh and a cry of, 'Mummy's boy!'

Prickle-Head.

I felt even worse.

But Dad looked up. He'd heard the laugh too. Prickle-Head didn't have *his* dad with him this time, only Pinch-Face. Pinch-Face saw my dad looking suddenly fierce. He said something to Prickle-Head. They both scooted off sharpish.

I felt a fraction better. But *only* a fraction.

'Cheer up, Tim,' Biscuits said. 'Dean and me were hopeless too. They laughed at us and all.'

But Biscuits had learned the knack of making people laugh *with* him. They laughed *at* me.

'I'm ever so sorry, Kelly,' I said humbly.

Kelly raised her eyebrows and sighed.

'So I should think!'

'You be quiet, our Kelly. Tim did his best,' said Kelly's mum. 'You were the mean one, rushing off like that and leaving him on his own. Anyway, it's only a bit of fun, kids.'

 179

'That's right,' my mum said gratefully.

Dad didn't say anything.

I knew he thought I was useless too.

I tried hard not to mind too much as the races went on and on. Nobody made me go in for anything else. But it didn't matter. I cheered Kelly and Dean in all their running races. They won. I cheered Biscuits in his sack race. He didn't win but he bounced along grinning all over his face so that everyone clapped nevertheless. I was pleased for him. But I still minded and minded about me inside.

Then the dads had a race. My dad ran like crazy and went purple in the face. Kelly's mum's boyfriend Dave ran like he was hardly bothering. And won.

My dad congratulated him but I could see he minded a lot.

Then it was the mums' race.

'I'm not going in for it,' said my mum.

'Go on, it'll be a laugh,' said Kelly's mum. There was nothing going to stop *her* going in for it, even though she didn't have the right sort of shoes to run in, just backless sandals with heels. She gave them to Kelly to hold and went to the starting post, practically dragging my mum with her.

I saw my mum's face.

I realized she hated sports just the way I did. She especially hated the idea of running in front

 180

of everyone and looking stupid. I felt a horrid new squeezing in my tummy. My mum was plumper than the other mums. And I'd seen her running for a bus. Her legs kicked out at the sides and her bottom waggled. I didn't want to see everyone laughing at Mum.

'This is going to be a laugh,' said Biscuits.

Then he saw my face.

'Hey, your dad gave you some pocket money, didn't he? Let's go and get an ice-cream from the van over there,' Biscuits suggested.

'OK.' I looked over at Kelly who was prancing around in her mum's high heels.

'Not her,' Biscuits said quickly. 'Just you and me.'

So we sloped off together while everyone else was waiting for the start of the mums' race. We bought an ice-cream each and stood licking them at the edge of the cliff.

We heard great shrieks and roars and laughing behind us.

I winced.

'Hey, let's have our own private Super-Tim and Biscuits-Boy race,' said Biscuits, swallowing the rest of his ice-cream whole. 'We'll have a roly-poly-down-the-sand-to-the-beach race, right?'

'Right!' I said, and then I stepped over the edge and started rolling right away.

'Hey! Cheat! I didn't say go!' said Biscuits behind me, as he hurled himself over the edge of the beach too.

I went roly-poly roly-poly roly-poly over and over and over, my eyes squeezed shut to stop any more sand getting in them. I bumped a few bits and went very wobbly but it was still fun, if scary. And I landed on the beach first.

'I won!' I said as I landed bump on my bottom on the beach.

'Look who it isn't! Old Mummy's boy!' came a dreadfully familiar voice.

But it sounded odd. Hollow. Sort of echoey and far away.

I blinked. I couldn't see Prickle-Head anywhere. Then I realized. He was in one of the sandy caves, burrowing away. I saw his great big boots and Pinch-Face's trainers sticking out.

I decided it would be wise to hasten back *up* the cliff sharpish.

'I'm second!' Biscuits shouted above me, hurtling down in a great flurry of sand.

He was sliding down with great thumps and bumps. And suddenly the sand all around him started shaking.

I stared. And then I shouted, 'Get out of the cave quick! The cliff is giving way! The sand's all sliding!'

Pinch-Face backed out so quickly that Biscuits

couldn't steer past him and landed bang on top of him. They sprawled in a heap, Pinch-Face groaning, Biscuits giggling.

'Where's Prickle-Head?' I said. 'Did he get out too?'

'Must have done,' said Pinch-Face, picking himself up.

There was a huge mound of new sand down on the beach.

'Wow! I caused a landslide,' said Biscuits, looking at the sifted sand. 'No, a *sand*slide!'

I stared. Something glittered in the sand. A stud. Several studs. Prickle-Head's boots! He was buried in the sand!

'Quick!' I said. 'We've got to get him out. Dig, you two. Come *on*. He's buried alive under all that sand. He'll die if we don't dig him free.'

I hated Prickle-Head but I didn't want him to *die*. We scraped and scrabbled at the sand covering him.

'Do his head end so he can breathe,' I said, but when we tugged his top half free his head lolled. His eyes were shut. I bent my own head nearer. He wasn't breathing.

'He's dead!' said Pinch-Face.

'I've murdered him with my landslide!' said Biscuits. 'Oh help, oh help, oh help, oh help.'

'Run and *get* help, what'syourname, Rick, *quick*!' I yelled. 'Biscuits, stop it! Keep getting the sand off him. Maybe that's stopping his breathing. It's crushing his chest.'

 183

'He's dead already, I just know he is!' Biscuits gasped, clasping Prickle-Head's horribly lolling head.

It suddenly reminded me of floppy old Dog Hog and the game we'd played in the car together on the way to Llanpistyll.

'Artificial respiration!' I said. 'Quick, Biscuits, do it!'

'I don't know how!'

'You did it with Dog Hog and Walter Bear.'

'I was just messing about. Oh Tim. He *is* dead.'

'Then I'll have a go at this kiss of life thing,' I said, as Biscuits scraped more sand off Prickle-Head.

I tilted his head back further so I could get at his mouth properly.

'Breathe into it then!' said Biscuits.

'No, wait,' I said, seeing all the sand around Prickle-Head's mouth. I shoved it open with my fingers and scooped lots of spitty sand out.

'Is he breathing now?' said Biscuits.

'Not yet.'

I stared at Prickle-Head's face, wondering how to do it. I need the mouth to stay open – and my breath to get down inside him. I pinched his nose to stop the air getting out, took a deep breath, and then breathed quickly into Prickle-Head's mouth. Then I took another breath and did it again. And again. And again.

Biscuits kept scrabbling all the while, clearing the sand.

 184

I breathed and breathed and breathed.

'It's not working,' Biscuits wept.

I went on breathing into Prickle-Head.

I breathed again and again and again.

Prickle-Head suddenly coughed.

I shot up from him. Prickle-Head turned his head sideways.

'He's being sick. Yuck!' said Biscuits.

'He's *alive*!' I said.

'Oh Tim! He *is* alive. I'm not a murderer after all. And you're a *hero*!' said Biscuits.

And then lots of people came running down the zig-zag path and more sand started sliding, so Biscuits and I dragged Prickle-Head completely free. We were surrounded by people and there was noise and pushing and questions – and then suddenly someone came charging through everyone, running even faster than Kelly. It was my mum!

She picked me right up and hugged me hard.

'Oh Tim! I thought it was you who'd been buried! Oh thank God you're safe. And Biscuits is too?'

'Mum! Put me down! People are *looking*.'

'I'm fine. And I do hope Prickle-Head is. Tim saved him. He gave him the kiss of life. He was wonderful!' said Biscuits. 'He's a hero!'

'Tim! Wow! You saved his *life*? What did you do that for? I thought you didn't like him!' said Kelly, barging

 185

through everyone. 'Still, you *are* a hero. My boyfriend Tim's a hero.'

'Oh son! Did you really give him the kiss of life?' said Dad, giving me a hug too. 'How did you know what to do?'

'I just sort of sussed it out. I didn't do much. I'm not really a hero,' I said, trying to wriggle free of Mum and Dad, scared everyone would start laughing again.

But no one was laughing now. Prickle-Head was carried up the cliff to be taken to hospital. He seemed reasonably OK now, though he had sick all down his front.

'That Tim rescued you. He gave you the kiss of life,' said Pinch-Face.

'No wonder I was sick!' Prickle-Head gasped.

He wasn't at all grateful! But I didn't care. Everyone kept saying I was a hero. And back at the carnival they gave me a special cup. It was supposed to be for the child that won the most races.

'But *you* must have it instead, Tim!'

'I'm ever so glad you're my boyfriend, Tim,' said Kelly.

'You're a *real* Super-Tim,' said Biscuits.

I don't know about that. I'm not *quite* Super-Tim standard.

But I'm Tim – and I *feel* Super!

HETTY FEATHER'S HOLIDAY

I changed out of my grubby work dress and cap and apron while locked inside the ladies' waiting room at the station. I felt better and braver in my emerald best dress, and my skimpy work clothes were much lighter to carry.

The third-class rail ticket cost a great deal of money, much more than I'd reckoned. The housekeeping jar was a lot lighter when I put it back in my case. It was very unnerving reaching Waterloo and having to negotiate my way up and down the platforms to find the correct locomotive for Bignor, but I managed it successfully.

I hadn't realized that it would be such a long train journey to the coast. I fidgeted a great deal as I gazed out of the window. England was much larger than I'd realized. I stared until my eyes blurred, but I still hadn't glimpsed any great expanse of water.

I opened Mrs Briskett's parcel for some lunch, and then carried on nibbling on and off throughout the journey. A grim-faced lady sitting next to me sniffed in disgust and twitched her skirts away from me, acting as if I were spilling crumbs all over her. It was certainly a temptation.

A much sweeter family joined the train at Arundel: a jolly father in a straw hat and blazer, a pale mother with a babe in arms, and two girls in sailor suits, one my age, one about eight or nine.

They all smiled at me, and the two sailor girls started chatting as if we were old friends, telling me they were having an early seaside holiday and it was going to be great fun.

I offered the girls a slice of Mrs Briskett's shortbread and talked to them a little. They were astonished when I said I'd never been to the seaside before.

'We go to Bignor every single year. We think it's the most splendid tip-top place ever,' said the older girl. 'We go bathing every day, and listen to the band and watch the pierrots. Oh, you will love it! Where will you stay? We always go to the same lodgings near the promenade. Maisie and I can see the sea from our bedroom window.'

'Where are your mama and papa?' asked Maisie. 'Are you travelling all on your own? How queer!'

'Maisie!' the mother rebuked her gently. She smiled at me. 'Are you going on a visit, perhaps?'

'Yes, to see my mama.'

'Oh, that's lovely, dear.'

'Why don't you live with your mama, then?' asked the older girl.

'Charlotte!' the mother said, shaking her head. 'You girls! Stop plaguing your new friend with your questions.'

'My mama works in Bignor,' I said.

'Your mama works! Why's that?'

'That's enough, girls!' said their mother, looking a little uncomfortable.

They weren't a very grand family. They were only travelling third class like me, and their clothes were a little shabby. I could see the telltale black line around the skirts of both girls where their hems had been let down, and although their boots were highly polished, they were cracked and down-at-heel. Even so, there was a huge divide between us. That little baby sleeping in the mother's arms would grow up safe within a family. She would be able to stay a child well into her teens. She would never be told it was her place to be a servant.

The baby was starting to get fretful, and wouldn't be soothed, though the mother rocked her tenderly. 'Hush now,' she said, over and over, but the baby wouldn't hush at all.

The father tried tickling her and then talking to her sternly, which made the baby cry harder. The girls

191

chatted to each other, clearly not expecting to take their turn as nursemaid.

'Let me take her,' I offered.

'I'm afraid she's very querulous, poor lamb,' said the mother. 'I'm not sure you'll be able to quieten her. Sometimes she cries for hours. I think it's the colic.'

I was used to little babies. In my last year at the hospital I had spent many hours in the nursery, helping care for the newborn foundlings before they were despatched to foster homes in the country.

'Come to Hetty, baby,' I said, picking her up from her mother's arms.

She had a cross red face, her forehead wrinkled as if she had every care in the world. The silly little thing did not know how lucky she was. I held her upright and pressed her against me, patting her back.

'There now. Do you have a sore stomach? This will make it feel better,' I said.

I walked up and down the carriage, rocking her against me. She stopped screaming, snuffled several times, and then quietened altogether.

'Oh my! You've worked wonders!' said the papa.

'You're very good with babies, dear,' said the mother. 'There, Charlotte, there, Maisie! See how nicely she's soothed your little sister!'

I took a deep breath, aware of a sudden glorious

solution to my situation. 'I would be very happy to be your nursemaid,' I said.

I meant it in all seriousness, but the family all laughed merrily, as if I were joking.

'I – I would not cost very much,' I ventured further, but this made them laugh even harder.

I felt I could not pursue the point any further. I continued to walk the baby. She stayed fast asleep, even when the train drew into the station at Bignor-on-Sea at last. I carried the baby very carefully down the steps to the platform, my suitcase hanging off one arm. The father went dashing off to supervise the removal of the family's luggage from the guard's van. I waited with the rest of the family.

Maisie was jumping up and down excitedly, declaring, 'I can smell the sea already!' She was so convincing that I imagined the water lapping against the brick walls of the station.

'I hope there's time for a bathe before tea!' said Charlotte. 'Will you have a bathe too? Wait till you see what it's like, Hetty! Do you have your own bathing dress? If not, you can hire one on the beach.'

'I expect I will do that,' I said.

'And you'll need a bucket and spade! Maisie and I always make sandcastles. It's absolutely ripping fun. We made such a splendid castle last year, with a proper moat, and then the sea came in and filled it

193

up, and we made stained-glass windows out of fruit drops. Maisie had to lick them first, which was a little disgusting, but she didn't mind at all—'

'Charlotte, calm down!' said her mother, smiling at her. She reached for the baby. 'Thank you so much for looking after little Flora. I've never known her so contented.'

'It was a pleasure,' I said solemnly. My arms felt very empty when I gave her back.

'Well . . .' The mama was looking around at the crowds on the platform. 'Can you see your mama anywhere? She will be meeting you, won't she?'

'Oh, she doesn't know I'm coming. It's a surprise,' I said.

'Do you know where to find her? Perhaps you might care to walk part of the way with us?'

'Oh, yes please!' I said.

We walked out of the station in a little procession, the papa alongside the porter, who had a huge trolley full of their luggage, then the mama and the baby, and then Charlotte and Maisie on either side of me, talking nineteen to the dozen, telling me all about the seaside.

'Where is it?' I asked, because we were in a perfectly ordinary street, though the light was brighter than usual and the air felt fresh and clear.

'Just down there! Oh, Mama, may we run ahead

just a little and show Hetty the sea?' asked Charlotte.

'Of course,' said their mama. The girls both surged forward, skirts flying. I ran along beside them, my case bumping awkwardly against my legs.

'Take care, girls!' she called.

I felt truly part of their family – not a nursemaid, more like a sister. I started picturing our life together. We'd have our annual jolly seaside holiday in Bignor, and then we would go back to our home in Arundel. I would go to school with Charlotte and Maisie, and help their mama with the baby when I was at home. We'd all do the cooking and the dusting and the scrubbing and the mending. I'd have my own comfortable little bed in the girls' room. I would never be stuck all alone in the scullery.

Charlotte and Maisie raced round a corner. I heard them whooping triumphantly. I followed them, and then stopped short, my heart thudding. I'd seen pictures of the sea in books, each wave carefully cross-hatched to give a life-like impression. I'd seen the Thames, which had seemed vast enough after the country stream of my childhood.

But nothing had prepared me for the immensity of this sea glittering before me in the sunlight.

I had fancied it would be a dense blue like the wash of colour in my picture-book illustration, but this was a bright silvery grey, an entire sparkling world of water. I turned my head to the left and to the right, and it was still there, as far as I could see.

I dropped my suitcase and stretched my arms wide, trying to take it all in.

'Isn't it glorious?' said Charlotte.

'Yes, it is truly wonderful,' I breathed.

The sea blurred to a rainbow shimmer because I was crying now, overcome by the beauty of this vast stretch of water. I scrubbed at my eyes with my handkerchief.

'Don't be sad,' said Maisie, putting her hand in mine.

'I'm not sad, I'm happy,' I said, laughing shakily.

'You do like it here, don't you?' she asked.

'I think it's the most beautiful place in the whole world,' I said. My heart rejoiced that Mama lived here now and could see the sea every single day.

☆ QUICK HOLIDAY QUIZ ☆

1. In *Candyfloss*, which country does Floss's mum want the family to move to?

2. What is the capital city of Italy?

3. Who invites Biscuits to go on holiday with him in *Buried Alive*?

4. Tracy Beaker believes her mum lives abroad. In which famous city?

5. What is the tallest mountain in the world?

6. What country is Berlin the capital city of?

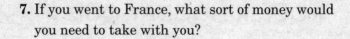

7. If you went to France, what sort of money would you need to take with you?

8. In *Cookie,* Beauty and her mum go to Rabbit Cove. What's the name of the little cottage they stay in?

9. In *Cliffhanger*, Tim finds a girlfriend on holiday! What's her name?

10. When Gemma goes to visit Alice in Scotland in *Best Friends*, what present does she take her?

WHAT'S THE COUNTRY?

'Mick's coming round on Saturday,' said Mum. Skippy smiled. She always smiles. If you told her the Bogeyman was coming to take her out to tea she'd clap her hands and smile.

I didn't smile. I can't stick Mick. I don't see why Mum has to have a stupid boyfriend at her age. She says he makes her happy. I can't see why she can't just be happy with Skippy and me.

'Mick's going to take us on a special day out!' Mum announced.

Skippy smiled. I very nearly smiled too. We didn't often get special days out.

I wondered where we might be going. A day trip to Disneyland?!

No, maybe not. But perhaps Mick would take us to the Red River Theme Park and we could go on all the really brilliant rides where you swoop up and down and it's like you're flying right up in the sky.

'Will he take us to the Red River Theme Park, Mum?'

'Don't be daft, Hayley,' said Mum. 'It costs a fortune. Mick's not made of money. No, we're going to have a lovely day out in the country.'

'The country?' I said.

'What's the country?' Skippy asked.

'It's boring,' I said.

I hadn't actually been to the country much, but of course I knew all about it. We've got this old video about kids living on a farm in the country.

The main girl in it is called Hayley like me. It's a good film but the country looks awful. Cold and empty and muddy, with cows that chase you.

I moaned, and Mum said I was a spoiled little whatsit, and I went into our bedroom and sulked. Skippy came and cuddled up beside me.

'We don't like the country,' she said, to show me she was on my side – though Skippy is always on everyone's side.

'That's right, Skip. We don't like the country. And we don't like Mick.'

'We don't like Mick,' Skippy echoed obediently, but she didn't sound so sure.

When Mick knocked at our door at nine o'clock on

Saturday morning, Skippy went rushing up to him, going, 'Mick, Mick, Mick!'

Skippy is useless at not liking people.

I am brilliant at it. And Mick was making it easy-peasy. He looked ridiculous. He always looks a bit wet and weedy, but today he was wearing a big woolly jumper right up to his chin and awful baggy cord trousers and boots.

Honestly. I knew Mum could act a bit loopy at times but she had to be barking mad to go round with Mick.

'Ready, girls?' he said, swinging Skippy round and round while she squealed and kicked her legs, her shoes falling off. 'Have you got any welly boots, Skip? I think you'll need them.' He put on a silly voice (well, his own voice is silly, but this was sillier). 'It gets right mucky in the country, lass.'

Skippy put on my old Kermit wellies and her Minnie Mouse mac.

'It's a Mouse-Frog!' said Mick, and Skippy fell about laughing.

I sighed heavily.

'What about your wellies, Hayley?' said Mick. 'And I should put a jumper on too.'

I took no notice. As if I'd be seen dead in wellies! And I was wearing the simply incredible designer T-shirt Mum found for 20p down at the school jumble.

I wasn't going to cover it up with an old sweater even if it snowed.

Mum looked like she wanted to give me a shake, but she got distracted looking for our old thermos flask. We were having a picnic. I'd helped cut the sandwiches. (Skippy sucked the cut-off crusts until they went all slimy like ice lollies.) The sandwiches were egg and banana and ham (not all together, though maybe it would taste good), and there were apples and crisps and a giant bar of chocolate, and orange juice for Skip and me, and tea for Mum and Mick. It seemed a seriously yummy picnic. It looked like I might be going to enjoy this day out in spite of myself.

Skippy and I nagged to nibble the chocolate in the car on the way to the country. Mum said we had to wait till picnic time. Hours and hours and hours! Mick said, 'Oh, let the girls have a piece now if they're really hungry.'

He rooted round in the picnic bag and handed the whole bar over.

This was a serious mistake. Skippy and I tucked in determinedly. By the time Mum peered round at us we'd eaten nearly three-quarters.

Mum was very cross. 'How can you be so greedy? Hayley, you should have stopped Skippy. You know she gets car-sick.'

'She's fine, Mum. Stop fussing. You're OK, aren't you, Skip? You don't feel sick, do you?'

Skippy said she didn't feel sick at all. She tried to smile. She was very pale, though her lips were dark brown with chocolate.

'Oh dear,' said Mum. 'Have you got a spare plastic bag, Mick? We need it kind of urgently.'

She was just in time. Skippy was very very sick. It was so revolting that it made me feel a little bit sick too. We drove slowly with the window wide open. I shut my eyes and wondered when we were ever going to get to this boring old country- side. I'd lost interest in the picnic. I just wanted it to be time to go home.

'Here we are,' Mick said cheerily at long long long last.

I opened my eyes and looked round. I hadn't realized the country was going to be so green. That old film with the other Hayley was in black and white.

'We used to come here on days out when I was a boy,' Mick said excitedly. 'Isn't it lovely?'

There was nothing much there. No shops. No cafés. Not even an ice-cream van. Just lots and lots and lots of trees. And fields. More trees. More fields. And a big big hill in the distance, so tall there were grey clouds all round the top like fuzzy hair.

'That's Lookout Hill,' said Mick. 'Right, girls! Let's climb it!'

I stared at him as if he was mad. Even Mum looked taken aback. He said it as if climbing miles up into the clouds was a big treat! We don't reckon climbing three flights of stairs up to our flat when the lift breaks down.

'Isn't it a bit too far?' said Mum.

'No, no. We'll be up it in a matter of minutes, you'll see,' said Mick.

Mick is a liar. Those few minutes went on for hours. First we trudged through the woods. It was freezing cold and dark and miserable, and I hated it. Mick saw me shivering and offered me his big woolly but I wouldn't wear it. He put it on Skip instead, right over her mac. She staggered along looking loopy, the hem right down round her ankles. Mum said she looked like a little sheep, so Skip went 'Baa-baa-baa.'

Then we were out of the wood and walking across a field. Skip went skipping about until she stepped in

something disgusting. I laughed at her.
Then I stepped in something too. I
squealed and moaned and wiped my
shoes in the grass five hundred times. We seemed to
be wading through a vast animal toilet.

'Stop making such a fuss, Hayley. We'll clean your
shoes properly when we get home,' said Mum.

She didn't look as if she was enjoying the country
that much either. Her hair was blowing all over the
place and her eye make-up was running.

'Now for the final stretch,' said Mick, taking Mum's
hand. She held onto Skippy with the other.

I hung back. I climbed up after them. Up and
up and up and up. And up and up and up. And up
some more.

My head hurt and my chest was tight and a stitch
stabbed my side and my legs ached so much I couldn't
keep up.

'This sucks,' I gasped, and I sat down hard on the
damp mucky grass.

'Come on, Hayley!' Mick called, holding out his
other hand.

'No thanks. I'll wait here. I don't want to go up the
stupid hill,' I said.

'You've got to come too, Hayley,' said Mum. 'We
can't leave you here by yourself.'

So they forced me up and I had to stagger onwards.

Up and up and up and up. I wasn't cold any more. I was boiling hot. My designer T-shirt was sticking to me. My shoes were not only all mucky and spoiled, but they were giving me blisters. If I was as little as Skippy I might have started crying.

'It'll be worth it when we get right to the top and you see the view,' said Mick.

What view? He was crazy. We were right up in the clouds and it was grey and gloomy and drizzling.

'Nearly there!' Mad Mick yelled above me. 'See!'

Then Mum gasped. Skippy squeaked.

And I staggered up after them out of the clouds – and there I was on the top of the hill and the sun was suddenly out, shining just for us, right above the clouds in this private secret world in the air. There were real sheep munching grass and a Skippy-sheep capering round like crazy. I stood still, my heart thumping, the breeze cool on my hot cheeks, looking up at the vast sky.

I saw a bird flying way up even higher. I felt as if I could fly too. Just one more step and I'd be soaring.

The clouds below were drifting and parting, and suddenly I could see the view. I could see for miles and miles and miles – the green slopes and the dark

woods and the silver river glittering in the sunlight.
I was on top of the whole world!

'Wow,' I said.

Skippy smiled. Mum smiled. Mick smiled. And I
smiled too. Then we all ran hand in hand down down
down the hill, ready for our picnic.

BEAUTY'S
HOLIDAY

We lugged our cases into the car and thanked Auntie Avril for letting us stay overnight.

'Well, if you get into totally dire straits you'd better come back, Gerry or no Gerry,' she said. 'And thanks for the cookies, girls. They were a lovely surprise. They're very good, Dilys. I thought you couldn't cook!'

'Mum's the greatest cookie cook in the whole world,' I said. 'And I'm learning fast, so maybe I'm the second greatest!'

We drove off, Auntie Avril standing on her doorstep under her hanging basket of petunias, waving and waving until we turned the corner.

'So, which seaside shall we pick?' said Mum. 'Brighton's fun.'

I remembered Brighton from a day trip. 'It's too big and busy and the beach is all pebbles,' I said. 'Let's find a sandy seaside place.'

'OK,' said Mum. 'Well, we'll drive due south and see

what we find. If we tip over into the sea we'll know we've gone too far.'

We couldn't go directly south all the time because the roads wiggled around and once or twice we had to stop the car and peer hard at the map. I couldn't read it when we were driving along because it made me feel sick. I wasn't much better sorting out the route when we were stopped. I kept squinting at red roads and yellow roads and little spidery black roads, trying to work out which one we were on.

'Don't worry, babes, we'll make it to the seaside somehow,' said Mum. 'Bournemouth's very sandy. And Bognor. Which one shall we aim at?'

I peered at the map. A name in tiny print suddenly swam into focus.

'Oh, Mum! Not Bournemouth, not Bognor. I've found a place here right by the sea and guess what it's called: Rabbit Cove! Oh, Mum, please let's go to Rabbit Cove!'

'I've never even heard of it. Let's see where it is.' Mum squinted at the map. 'It's obviously a very small place, not a proper town. I wonder why it's got such a funny name? You don't get rabbits at the seaside, do you?'

'I think it must be because of the shape of the cove. See those two sticking-out bits of land? They look like rabbit's ears!' I said.

'So they do! OK, OK, we'll go and have a look at

Rabbit Cove if you've set your heart on it, though I'm not sure there'll be anywhere to stay there.'

I tried hard to keep us on a direct route now, peering at the map as Mum drove, though I started to feel horribly travel sick.

'Open your window a bit – and sit back and close your eyes,' said Mum.

I did as I was told because all the world outside the window had started spinning and I kept yawning and swallowing spit. It seemed to be spinning inside my own head now. I was falling down and down and down into a scary black nothingness.

I called and called for Mum but she wasn't there. And then I called for Dad and I could hear him calling back. I struggled to get closer to him, reaching out, but then a light flashed on his face and I saw it was screwed up with rage.

'You don't want me and I don't want you, because you're ugly ugly ugly,' he shouted.

He shoved me hard and I tumbled on downwards, mile after mile, but I could still hear him shouting ugly. Other voices joined in. Skye and Arabella and Emily were shouting it, all the girls in my class, even Rhona, and I started crying, my hands over my ears . . .

'Beauty! Beauty, sweetheart, wake up. It's all right, Mum's here.'

I blinked in sudden dazzling daylight. Mum leaned over and pulled my head onto her shoulder.

'Oh, Mum, I couldn't find you!' I sobbed.

'It was just a horrible nightmare, darling, that's all. You were crying out and tossing about. I had to stop driving,' said Mum.

'We're driving?' I said stupidly. Then everything snapped properly into place. 'Oh yes, we're going to Rabbit Cove!'

'Yes, we are – and we're nearly there! You've been asleep a long time. OK now, pet?' Mum wiped my nose with her tissue as if I was two years old.

'I'm sorry to be such a baby,' I said, feeling ashamed.

'You're not a baby, darling! You're ever so grown up, much more than me. There now, let's get cracking. Rabbit Cove, here we come. Penny for the first one to see the sea.'

I sat up properly and we edged out of the layby back onto the road. I still felt a bit weird but Mum had the window right down and I breathed in deeply. We were on one of the yellow roads now, surrounded by fields of corn and barley, gentle rolling hills purple in the distance. And then I saw a dazzle of brilliant blue . . .

'The sea, the sea! I spotted it first! You did say a pound for the first one to see it, didn't you?'

'No, I didn't! A penny, you cheeky baggage.' Mum slowed down when we got to the next road sign.

We could stay on the main road and go to Seahaven – or turn down a little lane marked Rabbit Cove!

'OK, OK, we'll make for Rabbit Cove,' said Mum.

'You bet!'

'Don't be too disappointed if there's nothing much there, sweetheart,' said Mum. 'We can just have a little wander and then make for Seahaven. I think that's a proper seaside town so we should be able to find a little bed-and-breakfast place there.'

We turned down the lane for Rabbit Cove. There were tall trees growing on high banks on either side of us, their branches joining to make a dark green canopy overhead. Then there was a sign to a little farm, and then driveways to houses, then a whole street of little terraced houses with pebbles stuck on the walls. Then the shops started, a small supermarket, a dress shop, a little gallery, a newsagent's, an off-licence, an antique shop with a rocking chair outside, and a tearoom called Peggy's Parlour.

'Oh, we'll definitely go and have a cup of tea in Peggy's Parlour,' said Mum, giggling. 'It all looks so old-fashioned. I do hope Peggy herself is a little old lady in a black dress with a frilly white apron, tottering around writing everybody's orders in a little notebook tied to her waist.'

'You are daft, Mum. Don't let's go there yet though. I want to see the sea.'

'OK, OK, stop bouncing around in your seat!'

We drove on past a proper restaurant, a pub, and a white hotel with a big green lawn and several swings.

'See, there is a hotel! Oh Mum, can we stay there?'

'Maybe. It might be a bit expensive.'

'But Auntie Avril's given us heaps of money.'

'It might have to last us a long time until I manage to get a job,' said Mum. She nibbled at her lip. 'Beauty, what can I do? Jobwise, I mean. I've only ever been a receptionist, and I was hopeless.'

'You could do heaps of things, Mum,' I said. 'You could . . . be a cookie baker.'

It was a little joke to make Mum laugh. She smiled at me. 'OK, that's what I'll do,' she said.

She turned down a steep little lane towards the seafront. There were more houses now with sloping gardens. Some of the houses had signs.

'We could stay in one of these,' I said.

'OK, we'll pick one later,' said Mum.

We drove downwards, round another bend, Mum's foot hard on the brakes – and then we were at the seafront.

'Oh, Mum!' I said.

'Oh, Beauty!' said Mum.

Rabbit Cove was perfect. There was a high cliff on either side (the rabbit's ears) sheltering a beautiful cove of soft golden sand. There was hardly anyone on the beach, just a few families with little kids running about trailing seaweed and sticking flags in sandcastles.

An old-fashioned artist with a beard and a baggy blue shirt was sitting up on the little white wall, painting. At the other end of the wall there was a small car park, a little wooden hut for toilets, and a beach shop-cum-café festooned with buckets and spades and an old tin ice-cream sign spinning outside.

'It's just like a picture in an old story book!' I said. 'It's so lovely!'

I couldn't be sure I wasn't making it all up. I closed my eyes, counted to three, and opened them again. Rabbit Cove was still there, serenely beautiful.

'I'm so pleased it's lovely,' said Mum. 'I was hoping and hoping it would be and yet sure it would be this ropy old pebbly place, all grey and ugly.'

'Maybe I'm still dreaming?' I said. 'And you're dreaming it too, Mum.'

'Well, let's park the car and then we'll have a little run on the beach. If you can feel the sand between your toes you're definitely wide awake,' said Mum.

We put the car in the little car park. I delved into my suitcase for my drawing book and new felt tips and then we went on the beach. I kicked my shoes off and wiggled my toes in the soft powdery sand.

'I'm definitely not dreaming!' I said.

Mum kicked her own sandals off and did the same.

 219

'Doesn't it feel great!' she said. 'Here, roll your jeans right up, Beauty. We'll go and have a paddle.'

We ran across the sand, slowing as it became hard and damp, and then both of us shrieking as the first wave washed round our ankles.

'It's absolutely freezing!' Mum said. 'I think you can be the chief paddling girl, babes. I'll sit and watch.'

Mum sat back on the soft sand looking after my felt tips for me while I waded around up to my knees, jumping waves, stooping to search for shells, walking up and down the little ridges in the wet sand. When I went back to Mum I was soaked right up to my bottom but she just laughed at me.

'They'll dry soon enough. That's what the sun's for! Are you hungry, sweetheart? Shall we have a picnic? Wait here!'

Mum sprang up and went skipping over the sands, not bothering to put her sandals on. She went into the beach shop. When she came out she was carrying two huge whippy ice creams with a big carrier bag over her arm.

'The ice creams are for pudding but we'll have to eat them first or they'll melt.'

Mum sat down cross-legged and we licked our ice creams appreciatively. Each ice had two chocolate flakes and a little blob of raspberry sauce.

'They're a Rabbit Cove special,' said Mum. 'The

 220

chocolate flakes are meant to be ears and the jam blob is a little bunny nose.'

'Yum!' I said, eating all the distinguishing features of my rabbit face.

When we'd finished our ice creams Mum produced two cheese salad rolls, two packets of salt-and-vinegar crisps, two mini chocolate rolls, two apples, two bananas and two cartons of orange juice.

'This isn't a picnic, it's a veritable feast!' I said, clapping my hands. 'There's only one thing missing – cookies!'

'We should have kept a few of Avril's cookies. I'm sure she's not going to munch her way through the whole batch,' said Mum. 'Oh well, I'll have to try and make some more some time.'

We ate all our wonderful lunch and then Mum lay back on the sand, using her handbag as a pillow.

I trickled sand on her feet and she giggled sleepily, shutting her eyes. She was asleep in seconds. I wondered about burying her legs in the sand, but it was too soft and slithery to cling.

I tried to make a sandcastle, using my hands as scoops, but I needed the damp sand nearer the sea and I didn't want to leave Mum alone. I got out my drawing pad and felt tips and drew a sandcastle instead. I made it a huge sand palace with pinnacles and domes and towers. I had a sand princess with long golden hair peering out of her tower window, waving at the mermaids swimming in the moat around the castle. All the mermaids had very long hair right down to their scaly tails.

I had a blonde, a brunette and a redhead and then experimented with emerald-green, purple and electric-blue long wavy hair. I gave them matching jewellery and fingernails and thought they looked gorgeous, if a little unusual.

I studded the mermaid moat with starfish and coral flowers and decorated the palace with seashells in elaborate patterns. The princess looked a little lonely even though she had the mermaids for company, so I drew more people looking out of the windows. I drew a queen mother with even longer golden hair, a best-friend princess with short black hair, and a handsome prince with a crown on his floppy brown hair. He was holding a very special royal rabbit who had a tiny padded crown wedged above her floppy ears.

Mum turned on her side, opened her eyes and yawned. 'Have you been drawing? Let's have a look. Oh, darling, that's lovely! It's so *detailed*. I must have been asleep ages.' Mum sat up and stretched. 'Shall we go and have a little walk round and explore Rabbit Cove?'

We stood up and brushed ourselves down. We didn't have a towel with us to get all the sand off our feet but when we got to the little wall Mum sat us down and rubbed our feet with the hem of her dress.

'Here,' said the artist, holding out one of his painting rags. 'Use this. I've got heaps.'

'That's very sweet of you,' said Mum. 'This is a lovely spot, isn't it?'

'Yes. I must have painted it hundreds of times but I never get sick of it,' said the artist.

He was quite old and quite fat, with a smiley face and a little soft beard. He wore a big blue shirt and old jeans dappled with paint and surprising scarlet baseball boots.

'Are you admiring my funky boots?' he said, seeing me staring.

'I'd like a pair like that,' I said shyly. I stuck my feet in my own boring sandals and sidled towards him, keen to see his painting. It was very bright, the sky and sea a dazzling cobalt blue, the sand bright ochre yellow. I wondered if that was the way he really saw the soft grey-blue and pale primrose cove. He'd painted the children paddling, the families chatting – and right in the middle of his canvas there was a lovely blonde woman lying asleep, a plump little girl by her side, her head bent over her drawing pad.

'You've painted us!' I said.

The artist smiled.

'Oh, God, let's have a look,' said Mum, banging her sandals together and slipping them on her feet. She peered at the canvas, giggling.

 223

'Oh dear, you've painted me fast asleep!' She squinted closely at the painting. 'You've drawn me with my mouth open, like I'm dribbling!'

'No I haven't! And anyway, you looked lovely lying back like that.' He turned to me. 'You were drawing a long time.'

'Oh, Beauty loves drawing. She's ever so good at it,' said Mum.

'No I'm not,' I mumbled. I wished Mum hadn't told him my stupid name.

'Yes you are. I shouldn't wonder if she ends up a proper artist like you,' said Mum.

'I'm not a proper artist. I wish I was! No, I just like painting.' He looked at me. 'You've seen my work. Can I see yours?'

'Oh no, mine's silly. It's just made-up stuff,' I hedged.

'Go on, show him, Beauty,' said Mum.

I opened up my drawing pad and flashed my sand picture at him bashfully.

'Oh my goodness! Let's have a proper look.' He took the drawing back from me and peered closely at my picture.

'I know it's silly and babyish,' I said. 'I was just sort of fooling around. I know you don't really get rabbits with crowns and mermaids with green and purple hair. Well, mermaids aren't real anyway, obviously.'

'That's the whole point of painting though. We can imagine the world the way we want it,' he said.

'I think you're very talented, Beauty. Is that your real name?'

'Poor Beauty hates her name,' said Mum. 'You can call her Cookie if you like. That's her new nickname.'

'I think Beauty's much more distinctive,' he said. 'What's your name? Total Delight? Ravishing? Gorgeous?'

Mum laughed. 'I'm Dilys – but everyone calls me Dilly.'

'I'm Mike.'

We all nodded and smiled and then stood a little foolishly, not knowing what to say next.

'So . . . are you here for a day out?' Mike asked.

'We're here on a little holiday,' said Mum.

'Oh, lovely. You're staying here in Rabbit Cove?' said Mike.

'Oh yes,' I said.

'At the hotel or a guest house?' Mike asked.

Mum and I looked at each other.

'Sorry! I didn't mean to be nosy,' said Mike.

'No, no, it's just we haven't quite decided where we're staying yet,' said Mum. 'Maybe we should go and do that straight away, Beauty? Oh heavens, I hope they're not all fully booked.'

'It's not the proper holiday season yet. You should be fine,' said Mike. 'There's just the one proper hotel in Rabbit Cove but there are lots of bed-and-breakfast guest houses.'

'That's what we'd prefer. Could you recommend a particular one, seeing as you're local?' said Mum.

'I'll do my best,' said Mike. 'There's a row of them just up the hill in Primrose Terrace. I'll come with you if you like. I've finished my painting for today.'

He let me help screw up all the tubes of oil paint and fit them carefully in their box.

'I *love* the smell of oil paint and the way it's so thick and shiny,' I said.

'Have you ever used oil paints yourself?' Mike asked.

'No. Dad doesn't let me have paints,' I said without thinking. I wished I hadn't said Dad. It suddenly stopped being a holiday. I started to feel scared and sad all over again.

Mike was looking at me carefully.

'Tell you what – if you're around the beach tomorrow you can come and have a daub with me. I'll give you your own little bit of canvas, OK? Is that all right with you, Dilly?'

'It's very kind of you.'

We went to get the car, Mike walking with us.

'Do you think the bed-and-breakfast places will have their own car park?' said Mum.

'There's a little alleyway behind the terrace of houses. You can park the car there. I'll show you if you like.'

He got in the car beside Mum and directed her to the alleyway. It was a tight squeeze to get the car slotted in the space and Mum's always been rubbish at parking. She made one attempt. Two attempts.

'It's OK,' Mike said gently. 'How about swinging the steering wheel round, backing in – no, no, the other way!'

'Oh God, I'm hopeless!' said Mum.

'No, you're not. It's blooming difficult parking here. It takes ages to get used to it. Do you want another go – or would you like me to back it in?'

'You do it, please!'

Mike had the car properly parked in a matter of moments. He didn't crow though, he just shrugged and smiled when Mum thanked him. We got the two cases out of the boot, and Mike insisted on carrying them for us. I carried his paints and his art folder and his folding easel, feeling very important. I hoped people would look at me and think I was the real artist.

'OK, here we are, Primrose Terrace. Which guest house do you fancy?'

We gazed up and down the street. They were tall narrow Victorian houses painted in pretty pastels, pale yellow, pink, peach and white.

'Which do you think, Beauty?' said Mum. 'What about the one that's painted primrose yellow to match the name of the terrace?'

'That's quite a good choice,' said Mike. 'But maybe ...?'

 227

'There's the pink one,' said Mum.

'Not pink,' I said, and Mike nodded in agreement.

'OK, OK, the peach one. That's got lovely roses in the garden,' said Mum.

'Mmm. Maybe,' said Mike. He was looking towards the white house at the end. I laid his art stuff down carefully and ran to have a proper look at it. It had a shiny green door and green willowleaf curtains and there were white flowers painted on a sign above the door. I read the name – and came flying back to Mum and Mike.

'We have to stay in the white one at the end. It's called Lily Cottage!'

'Excellent choice,' said Mike. 'Let's see if they've got any vacancies.'

We walked up to Lily Cottage. I rang the bell.

We waited. I rang again. Nothing happened.

'They're obviously not in,' said Mum. 'Maybe we'd better go next door after all.'

'Or maybe I can let you in?' said Mike, producing a key. He put it in the lock and opened the door with a flourish.

'It's your house!' said Mum, laughing.

'It's how I earn my living,' said Mike, grinning. 'I've got a double bedroom free with an en suite bathroom and a sea view. It's my best room and very cheap. Come and take a peek. I hope you like it.'

It was a lovely old-fashioned room with a patchwork quilt on the bed, a rocking chair in the corner, two comfy armchairs with flowery cushions, a scarlet Chinese storage chest – and Mike's bright paintings all round the white-washed walls.

'We'll definitely take it!' said Mum.

'Make yourself at home,' said Mike. 'I'll go and put the kettle on. I'm sure you'd like a cup of tea.'

'I wish this was our home,' I said to Mum, when he'd gone downstairs.

'Oh Beauty!' Mum sighed and opened her handbag, taking out her mobile. 'I think we'd better phone home.'

'What? We're not going back, are we?'

'No, no. But it's only fair to let your dad know where we are. You're his daughter. I can't just whisk you away and not let him keep in contact.'

'Not yet though, Mum. We're on *holiday*.'

☆ SUPER SUMMER RECIPES ☆

ELSA'S BERRY ICES!

These sweet and refreshing home-made lollies are perfect for a hot summer's day. You'll need a blender for this recipe.

INGREDIENTS

(Makes enough lollies for you and all your friends!)
300g of your favourite summer berries, chopped into pieces (strawberries or raspberries are good!)
50g caster sugar
70ml water
A splash of fresh lemon or orange juice

DIRECTIONS

1. Heat the water in a pan until it begins to boil.
2. Carefully add the sugar and stir until it dissolves.
3. Add the fruit to the pan, plus the lemon or orange juice. Mix well.
4. Using a blender, whizz the mixture up until it's nice and smooth.
5. Pour the mixture into lolly moulds and add wooden sticks.
6. Pop in the freezer until solid, and enjoy in the sun!

STAR'S SCRUMPTIOUS S'MORES!

S'mores are an American treat that are perfect for a barbecue or a campfire! You will need long, thin metal skewers (or wooden ones, soaked in water beforehand) for toasting your marshmallows. Make sure an adult always helps when you are making s'mores, and be very careful around the flames.

INGREDIENTS

(Makes enough for ten people,
or five with a real sweet tooth!)
1 packet of plain digestive biscuits
1 large bar of milk chocolate
1 large bar of white chocolate
1 bag of marshmallows

DIRECTIONS

1. Break the chocolate into bite-sized slabs.
   (It's easier to do this when it's still in the wrapping.)
2. Take two digestive biscuits and place them on a plate.
   Then choose one piece of white chocolate and one piece
   of milk, and place one each on top of the biscuits.
3. This is the fun bit! Take a metal or wooden skewer
   and push a marshmallow onto the end of it.

Hold it above the barbecue or camp fire and turn it steadily, until the marshmallow has gone a lovely golden-brown colour and is starting to bubble and crisp!

4. Carefully push your hot marshmallow on top of one of your pieces of chocolate. Then place the other biscuit and chocolate slab on top and press down, making a yummy marshmallow sandwich!

TRACY'S TROPICAL SMOOTHIE!

You can put any fruit you like into this yummy drink! But for a really tropical taste, try pineapple and mango. Just like before, you'll need to use a blender.

INGREDIENTS
(Makes one big smoothie or two little ones!)
1/2 a mango, chopped into pieces
1/4 a pineapple, chopped
1 banana, chopped
A squeeze of lime or orange juice
1 heaped tbs Greek or natural yoghurt
2 tsp clear honey
3–4 ice cubes

DIRECTIONS
1. This smoothie couldn't be easier. Put all the ingredients in the blender and blend until smooth and creamy!
2. Pour into a pretty glass and decorate with a slice of kiwi or orange before serving with a straw.

GEMMA'S
HOLIDAY

It was great fun riding along in the Mercedes. Grandad kept calling me Lady Gemma and asking

me if I'd like a drink or a sweet or a rug around my knees. We stopped at a motorway café around six o'clock. We both had a huge fry-up of sausages, bacon, baked beans and chips. Grandad let me squirt tomato sauce out of a squeezy bottle all over mine. I wanted to write

Yummy nosh!

but it took up too much room, so I settled for

When we got back on the road Grandad tuned into a Golden Oldie radio channel and sang me all these old songs, telling me how he used to jive to them with Grandma. I sang too, but when the radio frequency started to fade I faded too.

I curled up on the comfy leather seat, head on a cushion, rug wrapped around me, and slept deeply for hours and hours. Then I was vaguely aware Grandad was picking me up, still wrapped up in the rug like a big baby in a shawl. He was carrying me into a dark house and tucking me up in a little camp bed.

I went straight back to sleep. When I woke up it was a bright sunny morning and I was in a totally strange bedroom, Grandad gently snoring over in the big bed.

I got up and had a little wander round the room. I peeped out of the curtains, expecting to see mountains and lochs and hairy Highland cattle and men in tartan kilts. It was disappointing to see a perfectly ordinary street of grey houses and a video shop and a newsagent and a Chinese takeaway just like at home. There was a man coming out of the newsagent's with his paper and a pint of milk but he was wearing trousers, and they weren't even tartan.

'What are you looking at, sweetheart?' Grandad mumbled.

'Scotland. But it doesn't look very foreign,' I said.

'You wait till I drive you to Alice's new house. It's right out in the country.'

'Can we go now?'

'Soon. After we've had breakfast.'

It was a satisfyingly Scottish breakfast cooked by Mrs Campbell, the lady who ran the boarding house. We had our breakfast in a special dining room with the other guests. Grandad and I had our own little table for two. I plucked at the checked tablecloth.

'Is this tartan?' I asked.

'Aye, it is indeed, lassie. The Campbell tartan, I expect. They're a very grand clan – especially the ladyfolk,' said Grandad, putting on a very bad Scottish accent.

Mrs Campbell didn't mind. She giggled at Grandad and gave us extra big helpings of porridge.

'You're supposed to eat your porridge with salt when you're in Scotland,' said Grandad.

'He can have the salt, darling, but you can have brown sugar and cream,' said Mrs Campbell, giving me a little bowl and jug. 'But leave room for your smokies.'

I wasn't sure what smokies were. They turned out to be lovely cooked fish swimming in butter. Mrs Campbell cut mine off the bone for me. Then she brought us lots of toast with a special pot of Dundee marmalade.

'I *like* Scotland,' I said.

☆ IDEAS FOR A RAINY DAY ☆

Stuck inside over the holidays?
Why not . . .

- Start a diary?

- Write your own play, cast your family as different parts, and host a performance at home?

- Paint your toenails in every colour of the rainbow?

- Bake your favourite cake?

- Pick your favourite Jacqueline Wilson character and write a brand-new story about him or her?

- Make a gift to give to your best friend the next time you see her, like a friendship bracelet or loom band?

- Test your memory skills? Ask one of your parents or a member of your family to place thirty different items on a table – they could be coins, books, toys, items of clothing, pieces of fruit, ornaments, or anything else. Look at the collection of things carefully, and give yourself exactly one minute to try to memorize them all. Then go into another room with a piece of paper and a pencil, and see how many you can write down!

- Visit Jacqueline's website and chat to other fans?

OUR FREE
DAY OUT

Where do you go for your summer holidays? Girls in my class camp in the Lake District or stay on farms in Devon or rent holiday cottages in Cornwall. Some of them go to Spain and come back celebrity brown, with their hair in little beaded braids. Several fly all the way to Florida and boast about braving Space Mountain and have autograph books with Mickey Mouse and Pluto signatures.

We don't ever go on summer holidays. We haven't got any money. There's just Mum and me and the three little ones. Bliss and Baxter are five and little Pixie is two. Pixie has big blue eyes and golden curls and everyone goes 'Aaaah!' when they catch sight of her. Bliss is quite pretty too, though she's so shy she always hangs her head so you can't see her face properly. Baxter looks fierce because of his crew cut

 243

but he is kind of cute. People always fuss over them because they're twins. No one ever fusses over me or goes 'Aaaah!' I'm ten, and I'm pale and skinny and I've got a frowny face because I worry a lot.

I was getting especially worried about Mum during the summer holidays because she was so fed up. She just lay on our battered sofa watching the television, not bothering to go out, even when it was sunny. Every time the kids yelled she'd wince and say they were  doing her head in. I tried to keep them quiet. I read them stories and we all did drawing together with my felt tips. That wasn't such a good idea, because Baxter drew a frieze of green monster men all round the kitchen wall, and Pixie decided to scribble with Mum's lipstick instead of a felt pen.

We played pretending games too. Don't laugh – I know I'm way too old for that sort of thing, but it was just to keep the kids happy. We played we were going to the seaside. I let the kids strip down to their pants and splash about in the bath for ages. They really liked that, but maybe it wasn't such a good idea either, because they splashed a bit too much, and the water seeped through the floorboards and dripped through the ceiling of the flat downstairs, and the woman from number six came up and had a shouting match with Mum.

'I'm sorry, Mum,' I said miserably. 'We were just pretending we were at the seaside.'

'Oh, never mind, Lily. She's a right moany old bag, that one. I know you didn't mean any harm. I wish I could take you all to the seaside. I'm going crazy stuck here day after day. It's not doing you lot any good either, cooped up in this little flat.'

We all went out to the launderette together. I helped out doing the washing, Baxter ran around with a plastic basket on his head being a Washing Monster, Bliss looked anxiously at her newly washed teddy spinning round and round in the dryer, and Pixie perched on an old lady's lap and chatted away to her.

'What a little darling!' said the old lady, whose name was Joan. 'But she's so pale. She needs to get some roses in her cheeks.'

'You're telling me,' said Mum. 'But I can't afford to take them anywhere.'

'My church is organizing some free day trips to the seaside – one for mums and kiddies, and the other for all us pensioners. The coaches are leaving from the bus station next Saturday. I think the kiddie special goes at eight o'clock, and I'm sure they've got a few seats left. Your kids could paddle in the sea, build a few sandcastles, and have fish and chips and ice cream.'

'Oh, wow, Mum!' I said. 'Please say yes. I'd love to paddle in the sea.'

'Fish and chips,' said Baxter, rubbing his tummy.

'Ice cream, ice cream, ice cream!' said Pixie.

'But we don't go to your church, Joan,' said Mum.

'Never mind. I'm on the committee, so I get to say who goes. And I say you lot go, OK?'

'Brilliant,' said Mum.

But it wasn't brilliant at all on Saturday morning. We're not very good at getting up early, especially in the school holidays. Mum set her alarm for seven, but then she slept right through it. I woke up at half past and shot out of bed.

'Oh no, we've slept in. We'll miss the eight o'clock coach!' I said.

'Oh, Lily, shut it. We'll get there in time, you'll see,' said Mum, staggering out of bed.

She got herself and Pixie dressed, while I chivvied Baxter and Bliss into T-shirts and shorts and got dressed myself. There wasn't time for breakfast. Mum gave us a piece of bread and jam to eat on the way, and Pixie sucked at her bottle in the buggy. We ran nearly all the way to the bus station – but it was nearly ten past eight now. We saw the coach disappearing in the distance without us!

 246

'Just my rotten luck!' said Mum, and she looked like she was going to burst into tears.

'Where were you lot then?' said Joan, coming up to us. She was wearing a pink sunhat and a pink flowery dress to match. 'Oh dear, oh dear, don't look so downhearted.'

'But we've missed our chance of a free day at the seaside,' I wailed.

'No you haven't, dearie!' said Joan. 'You lot will simply have to tag along with us old dears instead. Our coach leaves at half past eight. I'm sure there'll be room for you. I can always have little Pixie on my lap.'

So we had our free day out after all! Everybody else on the coach was over seventy. There was one little old man who was ninety-two and in a wheelchair, but Mum and the coach driver, Darren, helped haul him up into the coach. Darren wasn't over seventy – he was about Mum's age, very smiley and jokey, and he got all the old folks singing songs on the journey.

There were plenty of spare seats but Pixie sat on Joan's lap anyway, though she started fidgeting ominously when we were halfway there.

'I think Pixie needs to do a wee!' I said to Mum. 'Can you ask Darren to stop the coach?'

It was absolutely fine, because half the pensioners needed a bathroom break too, so we stopped at this roadside café. Then we were off again, and it wasn't long before we had our first glimpse of the sea. I'd seen it before, of course, but Baxter and Bliss were really thrilled, and Pixie kept yelling, 'Big bath! Big big big bath!' which made everyone laugh.

Darren parked the coach on the promenade and helped everyone down onto the sands. He took off his shirt because it was really warm and sunny. All the old ladies gave him funny wolf-whistles. Darren went as pink as Joan's hat and Mum giggled at him.

I helped Bliss make a great big sandcastle. We decorated it with seaweed and pebbles, and one of the old ladies gave us coloured toffee papers to make stained-glass windows. Baxter kept threatening to jump on it so I made him a separate big castle to demolish. Then he chummed up with an old man and they played football on the beach together. Pixie ran around all the old ladies wearing Joan's sunhat, and they all chuckled and called her a proper caution.

We all went into the sea together for a paddle. Even Darren rolled up his jeans and joined in. The dear old ninety-two-year-old couldn't go in the sea, so Baxter filled two buckets with seawater and he splashed his feet in them instead.

We had fish and chips for lunch, with ice cream for pudding. Pixie's cone fell in the sand, but nearly all the old ladies offered her theirs instead, so she ended up with an *enormous* amount of ice cream for one very small girl. I was in charge of Pixie while Mum went for a stroll on the pier with Darren. I kept a careful eye on her in case she was sick, but she didn't disgrace us.

Joan took lots of photos of us on our free day out and she sent us some copies as a souvenir. There's one of Mum, arm in arm with Darren, both of them laughing their heads off. There are heaps of photos of Pixie looking adorable in the pink hat with ice cream all round her face. Baxter and Bliss look great too, playing with their sandcastles. I usually *hate* having my photo taken, but there's one of me grinning right into the camera, my hair blowing back, my forehead not the slightest bit frowny because I'm having such a great time.

We never bumped into the other coach of mums and kids, but it didn't matter a bit. We had a much better time with Joan's friends. I'd still like to have camped in the Lake District or stayed on a farm in Devon or rented a holiday cottage in Cornwall. I'd have absolutely loved to have gone to Spain or Florida. But never mind – I bet I've had the best free day out ever!